Brothers of
Another Realm

Harry John Faulkner Jr.
and
Dick Swarthout

PublishAmerica
Baltimore

First printing

ISBN: 1-4137-6816-4
PUBLISHED BY PUBLISHAMERICA, LLLP
www.publishamerica.com
Baltimore

Printed in the United States of America

Dedication

The authors of this story offer it as a tribute to the memory of their friend and fallen comrade, Lieutenant Alan O'Brien, who gave his life in Vietnam while serving his Country.

Foreword

By Dick Swarthout

We met sometime in 1964 at Fort Sill, Oklahoma, while pulling our required tour of duty. Harry and I were part of a small group of guys who hung out together while at the Fort for the next year and a half of our young lives. We tried to be good soldiers, but made sure that we reserved enough time for recreation. As time went by, only Harry, Alan, and I remained. Then Harry was discharged and I followed two or three months later. Alan was left behind and lost his life in combat.

When I mustered out of the Army in March of 1966, I left with my wife and family for Boston, where my friend Harry lived with his new bride. My plan was to live in suburban Boston and go to work with Harry, but things just didn't work. So I left and went home to Alabama to begin the rest of my life.

My only contact with Harry was a brief telephone call I made to him some ten years later. Twenty-five years after that call and several months ago, he located me via the Internet and our friendship was renewed, this time for good. A couple of months after that call, my wife and I found ourselves in Bethel, Maine, where Harry had resided the past fifteen years. We surprised Harry and his lovely wife and spent the New Year's holiday with them. Many tearful memories were shared as we found that the love and respect we had for one another was still alive and well. We really hadn't changed that much (with the possible exception of our physiques).

We continue to communicate on a daily basis, primarily via email. In fact, we just finished writing a comedic adventure that is not quite ready for prime time—but we had loads of fun doing it. We are, on the surface, a study of opposites. Harry is from New England and I from, primarily, the Deep South. Yet, we have so much in common; we both were raised in Italian backgrounds and share a great passion for music. Our mutual sense of humor is nearly identical and loyalty is a big thing to us. Most of all, we still have this uncanny sense of oneness—as if we are always on the same page.

We still think often of our glorious times and adventures in the Army, when an unbreakable bond was formed. We both worked part time at night to augment our meager military wages. Harry was, and still is, a singer and had a lot of gigs in the Lawton area. I was a bartender and actually worked with Harry in the same lounge for a while, which proved to be an unforgettable experience. We are inseparable and I have always known that we would give our lives, if necessary, for one another. Since reuniting with my best friend, I have wondered what it would have been like if we had struck out on our own after our army days. What if…well, that's another story.

Chapter One

It was 1965 and it was wild. On the marquee in front of the Holiday Inn in Lawton, Oklahoma, it read: "DALE, DICK, AND HARRY—IN THE LION'S DEN."

The people behind the sign were Dale Cooper, a touring piano man and ex-gospel singer; Cpl. Harry Foster, stationed at Fort Sill, who sang with Dale; Spec 4 Dick Stuart, also of the local military post, and known as the "singing bartender."

Dick would occasionally leave his post behind the bar to do a comedy-musical sketch with Dale and Harry. They packed them in, as the saying goes, and they were living the time of their lives.

A song of the 80s would say, "money for nuthin' and the chicks are free"…and so it was during that autumn of '65.

It was around that time that Harry and Dick made a fateful decision. Harry was being discharged in a month or two, and Dick would be leaving the following February. They both had serious relationships with women and had planned to marry soon. Harry had the more entrenched relationship, in that his fiancée was his childhood sweetheart.

When Dick first met Harry, that's all he would talk about—his Mindy, his Mindy. As months went by and they did their "thing," it became apparent that Harry was beginning to experience other romances in Lawton. Women flocked to him and his golden voice.

One in particular caught his fancy and he fell in love all over again. He was torn between two loves. It was about that time when he realized he wasn't ready to give his life to someone else.

HARRY JOHN FAULKNER, JR.
DICK SWARTHOUT

Dick, on the other hand, was basically a one-woman guy. He had plenty of good times, but finally fell for a girl who worked at the inn with him. He thought he had met the one and only, but his jealousy of her made the relationship a stormy one. He was looking for a reason to end it, but felt he would never get over her.

Harry had done some serious soul searching when he and Dick met for breakfast that morning in October. After the usual exchanges of machismos, Harry asked his friend to listen to an idea he had been thinking about the last few weeks.

Harry wanted Dick to venture out with him and leave everything else behind at the time of their respective discharges. Dick, who admired Harry, would have followed him to Ethiopia if asked. He had never had a friend like Harry and quickly acquiesced. Both men realized that striking out on a new adventure would be the easy part. Parting with lovers was another matter.

Harry and Dick were honorable to a fault, and there was no thought of just simply disappearing. They were going to face what they had to do in a manly way. Harry would be first as he would be getting out the following month.

The days went by very quickly.

The day of Harry's discharge had finally come and Harry was strapped into his seat on the plane that would be taking him to Boston. The plane rumbled down the runway and soon left the sights of Oklahoma City to its inhabitants.

Harry looked passively out the window and thought of his rendezvous with his Lawton sweetheart, Renee, the night before. It was a tearful goodbye, to say the least and Harry began second guessing himself as he dozed off.

After changing planes in Memphis, Harry was on his way to Logan International and the waiting arms of his Mindy. It was a cold, gray day in Boston and Mindy and her mother were waiting for him at the gate.

God, how Harry dreaded this!

Harry watched the sky from the window of the silver bullet he was sitting in. The sky had been an awesome blue and filled with white puffy clouds when they lifted off from Memphis. They looked as though you could jump from the plane and just bounce and frolic on them like a big kid. They were beautiful. As the plane continued its journey northeast towards Boston, the skies that were so beautiful when leaving Oklahoma, had turned steel gray. The clouds became forbidding and treacherous looking. Harry wondered what it was like for the people on the ground living under these clouds on this particular day.

This particular day, thought Harry, ironically. *It is the day that I have been waiting for for two years. It should be the happiest day of my life, but now I'm dreading it more than any other in my life,* his thoughts continued.

He knew that on the other end of this flight was the hardest task he would ever have to undertake. He had to say goodbye to Mindy.

He had been with Mindy since they were both kids. He was fifteen and she was fourteen. They had seen each other every night except for the two-year hitch in the army. They had planned on getting married as soon as he got back from the service. They had been making these plans for the last seven years and now, it was ending. The skies outside the cabin of the plane had blackened and so did Harry's mood.

Mindy was waiting on the other side of the gate and watched as the silver plane spewed out its cargo. Down the ramp came the young people with long hair, as was the fashion in the 60s. They wore flowered shirts with giant collars and gold chains in abundance around their necks and "bell bottomed" pants. Old people were walking by and clucking about "how disrespectful these young people have become." Sailors, Marines, and Airmen were clipping down the ramp; all on leave looking for sweethearts and family.

Suddenly at the top of the ramp, almost the last one off the plane, stood a soldier. He was six feet tall with dark brown hair and deep brown eyes. He was fit and, in Mindy's eyes, the most handsome thing she had ever seen. She had loved this boy, now turned man, since her fourteenth birthday. She didn't know much about sex yet, but what she did know both she and Harry had learned about together.

Mindy was the product of an Italian family. She had lost her father when she was just a girl and it had left an impression on her that she would carry all her life. She was pretty with dark brown hair and a wonderful smile. She had a wonderful figure that could make Harry bless the fact that he was born a man. She had based her whole life on Harry. They were going to go through life together and live happily ever after. She had no idea that she was about to get her heart broken.

Harry saw that Mindy was, in fact, by herself. She had talked her mother out of coming to the airport.

Her mother was upset saying, "You just be careful. Don't you do anything stupid until you get that wedding band!" She was always terrified that Mindy would get pregnant before she got married.

It could have happened if Harry had his way, but Mindy was always strong enough to make sure that Harry never got "it" close enough to even consider the possibility of becoming pregnant. They could make each other "feel good" without actually "doing it." She was very excited.

Harry was striding up to the gate with such purpose and with such a serious face that Mindy knew immediately that something was wrong. It frightened her as she waited helplessly on her side of the gate. When he got to her side of the gate he reached for her and kissed her deeply and with such energy that it caused Mindy to flush.

"My, my, soldier," she said somewhat breathlessly. "Hold your horses until we get your luggage!" The smile froze on her face when she looked into his.

"We're not getting my luggage, Mindy," he said miserably. "I'm not staying. I have to go back."

"You have to go back?" she repeated. "Why? Are you going to Vietnam? Oh, God, please no…not Vietnam!" She began to cry. "I couldn't take it if you were over there!" she screamed.

"I'm not going to Vietnam," he said, softly. "I'm going back to Oklahoma. I can't get married now. I'm not ready for it yet. You and I are two good people who just want different things right now.

"If I were to get married right now, I would be cheating you and I would be cheating me," he said with palpable sorrow. "I can't do that, I just can't. I love you," he said softly, "but I gotta go back."

Mindy reached back with all of her hurt and disappointment and Italian anger and slapped him as hard as she could across his face. The slap made him wince, not only from the surprise of it, but the damned thing hurt like hell. Her eyes welled up with tears and she tried to say something, anything to save her dignity. He had embarrassed her and hurt her and she couldn't take it. She finally squared her shoulders, hardened her face, and turned and walked away without another word or even a look back.

Harry watched her back as she left and wondered if he had done the right thing. His heart was broken as well as he walked up to the ticket counter and presented his ticket for the plane ride back to Oklahoma.

The ticket agent looked puzzled and said, "Is this right, sir? You just got off that plane coming in from Oklahoma by way of Memphis and you're turning around and going right back?"

His question was answered with a sad smile behind sad brown eyes and a simple, "Yup."

Dick felt that his meeting with Brenda would not go well. He wasn't convinced that this decision was best for him, anyway. He would never mention this to Harry, but he was scared. He decided to meet her at the stables in the country where he had proposed to her some six months ago. He was sitting in the old '56 Chevy station wagon that one of their army buddies left Harry when he mustered out.

Brenda pulled up next to his car, and Dick motioned for her to join him. As she slid into the front seat, she asked," Kind of cold to go horseback riding, isn't it?" She reached over and pecked him on the cheek, but Dick was hard pressed to say anything in view of his thoughts of doom.

"I asked you to meet me here so I could talk to you about something important that concerns us," Dick choked.

Brenda, sensing Dick was having difficulty speaking, asked, "What's wrong, baby?"

"It's over," he blurted out. "I can't marry you, Brenda, I'm sorry!"

There was stone dead silence for what seemed like an eternity. Finally, she began crying. This made Dick feel even worse.

A moment later, the tears turned to anger and she accused him of running around on her and demanded to know about the other woman.

"That's not it, hon," Dick said while trying to soothe her feelings. "I realize now that I'm not ready for marriage. I know I need to grow up some more, see and do other things before I'll be ready to settle down."

There was more silence. Dick slowly pulled out his wallet and removed five one-hundred dollar bills. He gently put it in her hand and said, "Here, take this, it's all I have."

Instantly, and without hesitation, she threw the money in his face, got out of his car and got into hers. She glared at him through the window with more tears in her eyes.

Dick clutched the door handle and wanted desperately to run to her, but he knew he couldn't. It was over. Dick just watched as Brenda pulled away. He sat there in the old beat up station wagon and cried liked a newborn child.

Even though he needed the money, Dick quit his job at the Holiday Inn the next day. Brenda was working there as well with basically the same shift that he had. There was no way he could ever face her again. He had about three months to go and plans to make so he decided on trying to be a top-notch soldier for the rest of his hitch.

Harry had returned and was finishing out his gig at the Inn until Dick was discharged from the army.

It took the boys a couple of weeks to return to normal. Neither one was very good company. They met several times a week to discuss their plans.

One common interest they shared was their love of the water. They agreed early on that they would head for the water.

Dick wanted to go to Canada and work toward acquiring some land, so that one day they could jointly own a hunting and fishing lodge. Harry wasn't so sure about that plan. He was a little concerned about living outside the USA, for one thing. He enjoyed salt water as opposed to the smaller fresh water lakes and streams. Harry didn't necessarily want to return to Massachusetts, for a couple of good reasons. He sure as hell didn't want to be anywhere near Mindy, and he knew Dick didn't care for the colder climate.

Dick was sitting in the doctor's office on post for the routine physical exam before discharge. The military doctor asked Dick why he'd lost a lot of weight in recent months. He looked gaunt and weak, with protruding cheekbones and exposed ribs. Dick told him that he'd been burning the candle at both ends while holding down a civilian night job for the past few months. The doctor reluctantly cleared him for discharge but cautioned Dick to take better care of himself.

Dick had a bounce in his step and he was whistling as he walked out. All he had left to do was to clear post and he would be a free man.

Harry and Dick had a celebration dinner that evening at the best place in town. They spent several hours there exchanging ideas about what they should do and where they should go. It was all to no avail. As close as they were and with the many things they had in common, they simply couldn't make up their minds. That soon became a moot point, when their rotund friend with the voice of an angel, Dale Cooper, approached their table and joined them.

He said, "How would you two like to go to the Bahamas?"

Chapter Two

"The Bahamas?" said the boys.

"The Bahamas," said Dale.

"What the hell would we do in the Bahamas?" they both wanted to know.

They were intrigued by the idea though. It was a place that could satisfy a lot of interests for both boys. They would certainly be near the water which pleased both of them and it just never got cold down there.

"This guy has been coming to the club every night," said Dale, "and the other night he caught our act, with you and me singing, Harry, and Dick coming out from behind the bar. He thought it was not only funny, but showed a lot of talent. He is going to build a new casino down there and he wants us to work the main room," said Dale.

It was hard for Dale to control his enthusiasm as he spoke. He related to the guys that the man, John Sironna, seemed very much on the level and that Dale thought they ought to think about it.

"Where is this guy, John Sironna, from?" asked Harry.

"He's from somewhere in the northeast," said Dale, "Boston or New York, or maybe even Providence."

The answer piqued Harry's interest very much. He was all too aware of the men that were from Boston or New York or maybe Providence. Men who built casinos. He was also aware that you have to be careful how deeply you get involved with these people.

Dick was already to jump at the opportunity and Harry had some trouble chilling him out.

"Easy does it, buddy," said Harry. "It sounds like a terrific idea, but let me make some phone calls first."

"Oh, for Christ's sake," whined Dale. "All you ever do is worry about shit, Harry. What if he pulls the offer?"

"He won't if he is on the level," returned Harry, then continued. "If he is what I think he is, the offer will be good as long as we want it to be."

Dale and Dick looked at each other. Dale was confused, but Dick knew something was up and said, "Go for it, brother, whatever you think."

Dick and Harry had been together too long for Dick to start doubting that street savvy when it reared its head. He knew enough go let Harry go with his feelings and just play out until Harry's mind was put at ease. He closed the conversation with a simple, "Okay, Har, go for it."

Harry went back to his room at the Holiday Inn to make some phone calls. Dick went back to the base to finish some last minute business for clearing post and to get ready for the night's activities. Dale went home to get some rest before the night's gig.

Once in his room, Harry sat at the table that held the phone. He stared at the instrument for a long time and then slowly reached into his back pocket and pulled out his wallet. From the recesses of his wallet he pulled out a small piece of paper. It was rumpled and had been in Harry's wallet for the past two and a half years. He carried it through basic training and through his entire military obligation and never once thought to take it out and use the phone number that was written on it. The number was 617-555-1423 with the initials D.A. written in the lower right hand corner of the note.

There was a very small handful of people who had this number. It was the private number of Don Antonio Fastallo in Boston, Massachusetts. Just having this number in your possession could bring a RICO investigation around your head. It was both a privilege and a burden to possess this number. It meant that you had the Don's ear, but it also meant that you owed unswerving allegiance…

Many years ago in 1918, two brothers disembarked from the tramp steamer that had carried them from Sicily to America. The two brothers had been sent to America by two loving parents who understood that trouble was soon coming to Europe. They also knew the Italian government and knew, that in a war, the leaders would probably pick the wrong side. They wanted better for their two sons. It was with sobs and heartbreak that the mother of these two boys, Angelina Fastallo, put them both on the steamer headed for New York.

It was with pride that the father of these two boys, Enrico Fastallo, did the same.

The older boy, Enrico, named after his father in Sicily, was a very serious type. He believed in study and hard work and working within the system of this great country they had come to.

The younger brother, Antonio, named after his mother's father, was just as serious, but in a different way. He learned early, on the streets of Boston, that if you were tough and were willing to take chances, you could do all right in this new country they had come to.

It was inevitable that these two brothers would clash.

Enrico found himself always being protected by his younger brother Antonio. In schoolyard fights, it was Antonio who would get involved and, with great viciousness, end the fight for his brother.

It would infuriate Enrico, but Antonio would just say with a shrug, "Hey, nobody hurts anybody in my family. If they do, they got me to deal with and they ain't gonna like that!" It was this issue that would ultimately come between the brothers.

Enrico was in his final semester of law school when he came afoul of a certain Professor Jack Kelly. It came to pass on a beautiful spring day on the Boston Common that Enrico was studying for his finals. He had set out a blanket with food and wine and law books. He was deeply into sharpening his knowledge of Tort law when he heard music behind him.

The music came from the loveliest voice he had ever heard. It was the lilting voice of a beautiful redheaded girl of twenty-two years. Under that head of auburn hair were the most beautiful green eyes he had ever seen. The owner of these gorgeous eyes had the most wonderful white skin he had ever encountered. She was so unlike all of the Italian girls, with their olive-colored skin, who lived in his neighborhood.

"Are you gonna share that food and drink with anybody, or will you be keepin' it all for yourself?" said this angelic vision.

So unglued was Enrico that he spilled his wine and almost choked on the piece of cheese he was chewing. He had never encountered anything like this in his whole twenty-five years on earth. This vision of beauty with a hint of Irish Brogue about her and her deep red hair and, Oh, my God, those eyes, he thought.

"My name is Jacqueline Kelly," she said. "My friends call me Jackie. I would be pleased if you would call me Jackie." She went on.

"Was named after my father, I was," she said. "I do believe you know him. Professor Jack Kelly, the law professor. Your law professor, I do believe. I've been watchin' you go to class every day and I've been admirin' you." She went on with a confidence that betrayed her twenty-two years.

Enrico was in love. He was totally and completely in love. He would do anything to have this beautiful Jackie in his life. And it happened, just like that!

It never occurred to him that Professor Jack Kelly would do anything to make sure that his beloved daughter did not have this "Little Dago bastard" any where near her life.

What he did to make sure that it would never happen was to fail Enrico in all of the courses that he had with him. He did so unjustly and unfairly. When Enrico went to see him he was told by the professor that "no dago son-of-a-bitch is gonna get anywhere near my daughter and if he tries to, I'll beat him half to death."

He raged on at Enrico, "You might as well quit law school, you guinea bastard, because you'll never be passin' any of my courses as long as you dare go near my little girl! And if you don't pass my courses, you don't become a lawyer! It's that simple, you greasy little shit!"

When Antonio returned home that night, he could sense that his brother was very upset. He had to force the story out of him.

It was not like Enrico to pass on bad information to Antonio. He had to fear what his volatile young brother might do. Antonio had developed a reputation in the neighborhood for settling issues without respect for the law. The same laws that Enrico had come to love...

Professor Jack Kelly was winding his way back home from the local gin mill that he frequented almost every night. He was more than just a bit drunk and, as such, not a man to be trifled with. He was a big man and had earned quite a reputation as a street fighter and a brawler in the streets and alleys of Dublin, Ireland. A smaller man approached him on the street.

"Excuse me, sir," said the smaller man. "I wonder if I could speak with you for just a moment?"

Jack Kelly saw no reason to fear this little man.

"My name is Antonio Fastallo. Enrico Fastallo is my brother. I love my brother very much and I was wondering if you could help me out?

"My brother loves the laws of this country and wants nothing more than to represent clients and be a champion of those laws," Antonio started.

He went on, "I do not have the same affection for the law as my brother and you, but I too represent people in their grievances. For those who negotiate in good faith with me, things are good," he said, making his point very calmly.

"For those who don't see eye to eye with me...well, things are not so good." There was an edge of menace in his voice.

"I would be forever grateful if you could see your way to straighten out this misunderstanding between my brother and you."

This was said in a tone that made it clear that there was only one answer to this question and it had to be the one that this little man expected.

"Listen to me, you little Dago bastard! That brother of yours fails, do you hear me?"

It was a mistake made by a foolish man who had had too much to drink. He was much larger than Antonio and had a higher opinion of himself than he should have had.

"If he thinks he will ever get that olive oil dipped pecker anywhere near my daughter, he's got another think comin'. And I'll see to it that he never gets within a hundred miles of his bar exam. So you and your brother can go fuck yourselves!" He was screaming.

So intent was Jack Kelly on screaming at this man in front of him that he never saw the blackjack come from Antonio's pocket. It hit him with a thud that felled the big man instantly. Antonio continued to pummel Jack with the blackjack until he was barely conscious.

Jack's eyes were swollen and almost shut. His lip was split wide open and the elbow on his right arm had been shattered by a well-placed blow of the evil weapon in the hands of his tormentor. It was then that Antonio reached down between the man's legs and grabbed him by his manhood and squeezed until Jack's eyes began to tear and he was begging for mercy.

"If you do not take care of this situation between you and my brother by tomorrow night," Antonio hissed, "I will be back and this pitiful little cock of yours will be in your mouth! Do you understand?"

When Jack didn't answer fast enough, Antonio squeezed harder. "Do you fucking understand, you Irish prick?" he screamed in Jack's face.

"I understand," croaked Jack.

It was taken care of the next day. When Enrico went to thank the professor for taking care of the misunderstanding, he was shocked to see the condition the professor was in. The bruises and the cast on the right arm up to the elbow horrified Enrico. He knew without being told what had happened. It was the last time he ever spoke to his violent brother.

When Enrico passed the bar, on his first try, the first thing he did was change his name from Enrico Fastallo to Harry Foster. He wanted no connection between him and his brother. He was the law and his brother, Antonio, was the anti-law. It was that simple.

When Harry Foster, Sr. died many years later, a very serious looking man at the wake called Harry Foster, Jr. by his Old World name and pressed a letter into his hand. Harry didn't recognize the man.

"Enrico," said the man, "this is from your Uncle Antonio." After slipping the letter to Harry, the serious looking man just walked away without looking back.

On the outside the letter was addressed to Harry Foster Jr., but on the inside the letter was addressed to Enrico Fastallo Jr.

The letter said, "If you need me, call me." It was signed…Uncle Antonio.

This was the man who answered the phone call from the Holiday Inn in Lawton, Oklahoma.

"Pronto," said the voice.

"Uncle Antonio? It's Harry…"

"Enrico!" said the voice with obvious pleasure, "It is so nice to hear your voice, my nephew. What can I do for you?"

Chapter Three

It was colder than hell that February morning when Dick and Harry pulled out of Lawton. It had been an incredibly bad winter in 1966. Harry headed the old Chevy up the Bailey Turnpike toward Oklahoma City. It had been a couple of weeks since Harry's Uncle Antonio found out that Siranno was a sham. It was only through Harry's pleadings to his Uncle Antonio that Siranno was still walking around somewhere. There had been no real harm done, other than raise false hopes of three innocents. They had said their goodbyes to Dale, who couldn't thank Harry enough for exposing the con man.

They had about $1200 bucks between them as they continued motoring north. They had planned to head for Chicago and find work, save some money, and try to decide what they would do with their young lives. It was three p.m. when they hit Tulsa.

"You hungry?" Harry asked.

"Yeah, I could eat," Dick replied.

Harry wheeled the wagon into the parking lot of a Dairy Queen where they had lunch and smoked a couple of cigarettes.

"Harry, what do you think about college? I mean, don't you think we could do better for ourselves in the long run if we got a college degree?"

"I can't argue with that, man," Harry replied, "but it would be a bitch."

"Yeah, I guess so. Maybe we should concentrate on getting some dough put together for right now. I dunno," Dick said, almost to himself, as they pulled back out in traffic.

Nothing else would be said on the subject for quite some time.

The trip proved uneventful and they checked into a motel in Cicero the following evening. It took three days, but Dick found a bartending job in a college hangout in Evanston, about three blocks away from Northwestern University. The bar was called Wild Thing and doubled as a haunt for aspiring new artists. It wasn't long before Harry made his presence known there. He was very popular with only an acoustic guitar for accompaniment.

He and Dick had located a small flat within a mile from campus, and things were falling into place nicely, although they weren't exactly making a killing.

Then, of course, there were the women. They came in all sizes and most had IQs of 120 plus. You didn't get into NWU otherwise. It was the best of times, part two. The boys wore themselves out most every night, and couldn't have been happier.

It didn't take long for Harry's reputation to spread around the north side of Chicago. The Wild Thing was absolutely jam packed on weekends and full the rest of the time. Fearing he might leave, the owner gave Harry a nice salary increase, but Harry insisted that Dick get one also. The owner did not have much of a choice, given the present circumstances, so he went along. Dick learned of this from the owner, who said something to the effect that "your friend drives a hard bargain," Dick was embarrassed, but also very grateful, as it was becoming hard to make ends meet in the affluent part of town in which they resided. That night, Dick thanked Harry for getting him the extra money. "I know that there are few friends that would do for me what you did today, Harry." But then, this was the way it had always been between the two.

Months went by and on one Saturday night, after Harry completed his last set, a fastidiously dressed man approached and said, "Mind if I sit down?"

"Sure, be my guest," Harry replied.

"My name is Jocko Dunn," the stranger said, "and I like your style."

"Thanks, pal. Glad you dig it," Harry replied.

"I've got a four piece combo called the Nomads," said Jocko. "We play in Chicago, near the lake at a place called The Sandpiper."

"That's cool, man," Harry, said. "What can I do for you?"

"Well," the man named Jocko said, "we just lost our lead singer two days ago and we're looking for a permanent replacement. I was just wonderin' if you might be interested in auditioning with us."

Harry, doing his best to hide his excitement and appear older than his twenty-three years, replied, "Might be, Mr. Dunn…what do you play?"

"Oh, we play a little jazz, some big band stuff. A little bit of everything, really," Jocko stated.

Again, trying to be real smooth about all of this, while sweating like a hog, Harry said, "Yeah, I might be interested in giving it a try."

"Good," Dunn said. "Meet me at the club at eleven a.m. tomorrow. I'll introduce you to the boys and we'll jam a little. If it fits, we'll talk money, okay?"

"I'll be there, Mr. Dunn," Harry replied.

"See you, and call me Jocko," he said as he left the premises.

Dick had been cleaning up behind the bar while this was all going on and had kept an eye on the stranger while he had conversed with his friend.

"What's going on, Harry? What's with the 'Man from Glad'?" Dick asked.

Harry went on to fill Dick in with the details, and Dick was just as excited as Harry. Neither of them slept much that night.

The Sandpiper was just off State Street, running away from the lake. It was an upscale place. Although not a large venue, it wasn't small, either. Harry liked the seating and lighting, in particular. It gave the place a look of elegance without being intimidating to the average Joe. *The bandstand was a little small*, Harry thought, *but it was larger than The Wild Thing setup.*

"Hey, Harry," a voice behind him echoed. He turned and saw Jocko coming toward him, again in high fashion. Then as Jocko reached where Harry was standing asked, "Hey, Harry, waddaya think of the place?"

"Nice, real nice, Jocko," Harry answered.

The three other band members appeared from the shadows.

"Harry, meet Frank Lane, drums...Lou Bellino, bass...and Dusty James, lead guitar."

They all exchanged the normal pleasantries and Harry thought that they were friendly enough, but not gushy. They were just friendly enough to let him know he might fit...but maybe not, They were all pretty fond of the lead singer they had just lost.

Jocko eased in behind the piano while the others prepared. "You know 'One More for the Road'?" he asked.

"Yeah," Harry said, "in the key of E."

In a moment, they began. Harry was a little cautious at first, but quickly got the feel of the group and then they were grooving. *These guys are good,* Harry silently thought, and he felt as though they made him better than he really was.

When they finished, Jocko said, "Now, let's go up-tempo...'Kansas City'," he shouted, and the fun began. They played for over an hour and Harry couldn't remember when he had this much fun.

"Okay, fellows, that's it for now. Harry, have a seat over there and I'll be right with you," the dapper bandleader said. Several moments later Jocko joined him at the table.

"Harry, how'd you like to be in the band?" asked Jocko. "Before you answer, here's what we're prepared to pay you."

Dunn scratched a figure on a bar napkin and shoved it over to Harry. Harry thought he did a good job in hiding his inner glee when he saw that the figure was TWICE what he was making at The Wild Thing, even with the new raise he'd just received. It was five nights a week, eight to three in the morning.

Harry looked Jocko in the eye and said, "I'll take it, Jocko," in his best Tony Bennet demeanor.

There was no way he could give The Wild Thing a proper notice, which greatly pained Harry. The Nomads needed him right away and he had to do what he had to do. He had discussed it with Dick when he arrived back at the apartment and, of course, Dick was ecstatic over the news, but at the same time, sad that he wouldn't be working with Harry every night. They went out to dinner that night, as it was one of their days off. It was over dinner that Dick informed Harry that he had enrolled in classes at the university. He thanked him again for getting him the raise, because that, in conjunction with a GI loan, had made it possible. They both got very drunk that evening, while celebrating their mutual good fortunes.

Harry told his boss he was leaving the next day, much to the owner's chagrin. Harry told Dick that he would be needing exclusive rights to the old Chevy in order to get to and from his job each evening. That was okay as far as Dick was concerned, since they lived within walking distance to Dick's work as well as the campus.

It was a Wednesday night when Harry reported for his first night at The Sandpiper. There was a small crowd when he arrived and he made his way to the dressing room. He had learned that the Nomads had been together for over two years and had been the Chicago area for the past six months. They were on the third week of a six-week gig at The Sandpiper, and Jocko also functioned as their agent. All the guys looked to be in their mid-thirties, except Lou, who appeared to Harry to be about fifty.

"It's show time!" Jocko hollered, and the group, including the newest addition, Harry Foster Jr., filed out of the dressing room and made their way to the stage. The crowd, although sparse, really got into it that Wednesday night, and Harry started building a new reputation from that night on.

Dick was struggling to stay awake in his English Lit class that morning. It had been three months since he'd started and the first big snow had hit the Windy City. He and Harry had been in Chicago for thirteen months now and were finding out what it meant to be on your own, with no First Sergeant to tuck them in each night.

Dick's grades had been decent, although he felt he could do better if he had more time to study. He hadn't opted for a major because he hadn't decided what he wanted to do yet.

Harry was a smashing success downtown…so good, in fact, that the band had been given a three-month extension on its contract. In recent weeks, Jocko had been fielding offers from all over Chicago, and it looked as if the group was headed to bigger things…and soon. Dick and Harry seemed to be growing further apart with each passing day. They seldom spoke to each other due to Dick's absence during most of the day while attending school and lengthy stints studying in the library.

One evening when Harry was off, he dropped in on his friend at The Wild Thing. He walked up to the bar and spoke to Dick, "Hey stranger, how have you been?" he asked.

"Just keep burnin' the candle at both ends, Harry," said Dick.

Harry tossed the keys to the Chevy to Dick and said, "She's all yours now, buddy. I've got another set of wheels now."

HARRY JOHN FAULKNER, JR.
DICK SWARTHOUT

Dick took a break and walked outside and saw a red 1966 GTO that took his breath away. Harry opened up the passenger door and asked, "Wanna ride?"

"Damn, Harry! What a ride!" Dick exclaimed. To himself he thought, *Only here about a year and already driving a new Goat.* Then, aloud, "No, Harry, can't get away from the store right now, but I'll sure take a rain check," Dick advised.

"Okay, man. Gotta scoot. I got a hot date tonight."

Harry got on the Goat hard as he pulled away and power-shifted up the street. He left Dick standing there feeling envious and inadequate, but Dick was still very proud of his friend and what he'd accomplished in the relatively short time he'd been in Chicago.

During the next thirty days, Harry and the Nomads, as they were now named, would find a bigger gig and Dick would lose a roommate.

Chapter Four

Dick took to college like a duck to water. It wasn't long before he was on the Dean's List and he was being asked to tutor other students. He was a natural. He was a few years older than most of the students because of his stint in the U.S. Army and as such, he was a bit more serious than they were.

He had decided on a pre-law course. He had always been fascinated by the nuances of the law and thought that he might be good at it. He always loved a good argument and felt that it just couldn't get any better than this. You could argue a point and get paid for it! Go figure.

It had been four years since he and Harry had parted. They stayed in constant contact with one another and remained the best of friends. Harry and the Nomads were doing really well in show business and they were a big name in Las Vegas. It was at least twice a year that Harry sent tickets up to Dick to fly down and stay, as his guest, for a week or so.

Harry would set him up with a bartender's job for the summer and they would room together like the old days. In Vegas a bartender makes a tremendous amount of money. This was how Dick paid for college and all of his expenses. The G.I. Bill benefits ran out after regular college.

To say that they were rooming together like the old days was a bit misleading. Harry's digs had improved quite a bit since the old days. He had been playing the big lounges in Vegas for three of the last four years and his surroundings showed it. He had lots of "stuff."

He had new cars and wonderful clothes, but his crowning achievement was his home. It was a one-level stucco ranch out in the desert. It had an Olympic sized swimming pool, six baths, and fourteen bedrooms. The kitchen was a professional kitchen with every kitchen tool and toy imaginable. Harry loved to throw parties and he always did all the cooking himself.

The master suite was magnificent. It was located at the very end of the house and as such was very much secluded from the rest the goings on anywhere in the rest of the house. It was of enormous size and it had a bath that included a whirlpool large enough for four people which, on occasion, was needed. It had a walk-in shower that had six water jets poised to rinse and pulsate all over the bather's body. It was done in earth tones and the counters and sink tops were real New Hampshire granite, polished to a high gloss.

The sleeping area was something to behold. Over the bed there was a large skylight that looked up to the heavens. On a clear night, which in the desert was almost always, Harry could look up through the skylight at God's palette and see things that were so beautiful and so awe-inspiring that it made Harry feel very small.

The bed was handmade by Harry. It was made of Maine ash with inlays of rosewood applied in a pattern that looked like the desert view outside Harry's window. This room, too, was decorated in earth tones.

It was now 1974 and Dick had just come down from Chicago. He had in his hands his degree from NWU Law School, and his Certificate of Passing from the Illinois Bar. He was a full-fledged lawyer now. He had graduated at the top of his class and was ready to go to work. It was at this point that Harry made a suggestion that would change their lives once again.

"Dick," said Harry. "I've just been contacted by Fortune Studios and they want me to do a movie. It's about a guy who wants to go into show business, and all the trials and tribulations that he goes through. I don't think I'll have to reach too deep to do this one," he added with a bemused smile.

"Harry, that's fuckin' great!" shouted Dick. "I can't believe it! Harry Foster Jr, a fuckin' movie star! Can you believe this shit? Oh man, when does it start?" Dick asked with incredulity.

"Well, see that's the thing. I'm not sure when it will start because I don't have a representative. I don't have somebody I can trust out there watching out for my interests. In all the years that I've been in show business I have never had an agent nor have I ever had a lawyer!"

"Oh no," said Dick, almost as if he had been hit with a cattle prod. "No Godamned way!" he said, backing away from Harry. "Harry, for God's sake, I just passed the bar! Are you fuckin' nuts!"

"Listen to me, Dick," demanded Harry. "I don't care how long you've been a lawyer. I trust you! That, to me, is worth more than all the experience in the world. For Christ's sake, Dick! Cross some t's and dot some fuckin' i's! Come on now! How tough could it be?"

"How tough can it be?" insisted Dick. "It can be tough enough so that you get screwed if I do it wrong!" warned Dick. "I'm sorry, man. I won't do it. I can't do it for God's sake. I haven't been a lawyer for a whole month yet," lamented Dick. "Harry, you have no idea what you are asking me to do!"

"Are you through, yet?" asked Harry.

"Whaddya mean am I through, yet?" Dick hollered back.

"Are you through bitchin' and whinin' and wailin' yet?" Harry asked quietly.

31

"No, you don't, you son-of-a-bitch!" screamed Dick. "You got that 'quiet thing' goin' and I'm not buying it! You and your God damned mafia personality. Don Enrico, the shithead! I ain't doin' it, you pain in my ass. I'm not doing it. So you can stuff that bullshit 'quiet man stuff'!"

"Flight 515 is now boarding for Los Angeles at Gate 5," said the woman with the perfect diction and tone over the airport speaker system.

A well-dressed and sharp looking man strode to the gate with a first class ticket in his hand. "Welcome aboard Flight 515, Mr. Stuart. I hope your flight to Los Angeles will be enjoyable."

'Yeah, yeah, yeah," said Dick Stuart as he boarded the plane.

Chapter Five

The sleek black Lincoln limo with the studio's logo affixed on each door was awaiting Dick outside the airport doors. The driver opened the rear door and Dick slid into absolute luxury.

As the driver got underway, Dick was thinking about the last two weeks. Harry had taken his screen test with Fortune Pictures, and it was a successful shoot. Dick couldn't believe he let Harry talk him into this deal—but then again, it was a matter of loyalty. Had it not been for Harry's support and assistance over the last two years, he would still be in law school. He knew he owed him big time. What the hell, he had to get his feet wet sometime, he had rationalized, even though he had envisioned himself in the corporate offices of some industrial giant. He had done well in gaining the degree in Business Law and he supposed this action would be a good first step…and the pay wasn't too shabby, either…15%. He could use the money…he had some loans to repay and needed to find living accommodations commensurate with his new social status.

Within the hour, he found himself face to face with Wade Hardy, Director of Planning at Fortune, along with Studio Counsel, a Mr. Brad Winthrop. Hardy reviewed the results of the screen test that Harry had done and was prepared to offer him the leading role in a film with the working title, *28 Hours A Day*. Privately, Dick thought the title had a cheesy air about it, but was aware that in Hollywood a working title seldom was used in the finished product. Hardy offered a compensation package that fell somewhat short of what Dick had in mind, but this was soon resolved to his satisfaction after negotiating for a short time. What caused a snag in discussions were the lack of overseas rights and a percentage of the gross gate that Dick had proposed on behalf of his client. They talked for over an hour and, despite the fact that negotiations were cordial, it became clear the two sides were at an impasse. It was then that Dick upped the ante in this poker game.

"Gentlemen, I think we're spinning our wheels and it's time to adjourn. I'll be staying at the Beverly Hills Hilton until ten a.m. tomorrow. You can reach me there should you reconsider. Good Day."

Dick had put Harry's and his own ass on the line with that move, and he knew it as he strode out of the office door after first shaking hands with the two men. Dick thought they were probably asking each other after he left, "Who is this asshole?"

Dick went straight to the hotel and placed a call to Harry. Harry wasn't in at the time, so Dick left a message on the answering machine. He took a shower and had something sent up to the room to eat. He didn't want to miss Harry's call.

A half an hour later the phone rang and it was his client on the other end. "Counselor, how are things going out there," Harry asked.

"Dunno yet, Har…we've hit a stumbling block," Dick replied.

When he gave Harry the details of the day's meeting, there was a moment of silence. "Uh, Dick, are you saying they offered us 600 grand and you walked out on 'em!?"

"Well, ah, yes, actually I did, Harry, but…"

Dick was unable to get the rest of his explanation out before Harry yelled, "Dick! What were you thinking? "That's more than I make out here in three damned years!!!!!"

"I know, I know, Harry, but…" Dick began to say.

Harry was too angry to listen. "You get them on the phone and make the damn thing fly right now!" Harry demanded.

Dick paused, and then said in an even voice, "I'll do as you want, Harry, but in my opinion, you'd be making a mistake. You deserve a bigger piece of the pie than they're offering. I've researched the industry compensation structure for the past two weeks and feel what I'm asking isn't out of line." After a brief pause, Dick added, "Harry, if you wanted to handle this, why did you insist on getting ME to do it?"

Another pause, and finally, "Dick, handle it your way…I gotta go to work now," Harry tersely replied.

"Goodbye." That was it.

When Dick hung up, he sat down on the edge of the bed and thought, *I knew I shouldn't have mixed business with friendship.*

The ringing of the telephone early the next morning awakened Dick. The call was from Winthrop, the lawyer for Fortune films.

"Can you meet with me at the Embers on Vine at ten this morning?" asked Winthrop.

"I suppose so. Why?"

The lawyer replied, "We have a counteroffer to your proposal."

The plane ride from LAX back to Las Vegas took less than an hour and in another half hour Dick was sitting in Harry's luxurious living room. Harry, who had just awakened after a full night of work and partying, wasn't fully awake when Dick handed him the legal documents to peruse.

"Just tell me what's in it, Dick."

"Well," Dick said, "you know about the money, but what's more important is the gate percentage and overseas rights. We didn't quite get what I wanted, but I think that the final package is fair. He then added. "I estimate that the fringes should double your movie salary, assuming the film has a reasonable run." Dick had a self-satisfied look on his face.

Harry was fully awake and his eyes were wide open. "Dick, I don't know what to say. I feel like such a jerk for the way I talked to you yesterday." Harry was obviously humbled by what his friend had accomplished in Los Angeles.

"It's okay, Harry, I understand. In fact, for a while I was second guessing myself," Dick replied graciously.

Harry embraced Dick, and whispered, "You're like a brother to me. I will never doubt you again."

There was much work to do before Harry left to start filming in two weeks. He had to perform in Las Vegas right up to his departure. He was also trying to absorb the script he'd been sent from Fortune.

Dick was frantically trying to find some nice real estate in Las Vegas, but decided against it for the time being, at least until he helped Harry get through the initial stages of making the film. In addition, he hadn't decided for sure where he wanted to live.

Harry had found the Nomads a good job in Phoenix after he left Las Vegas and left them a little something extra in their Christmas stockings. He was a very generous man and always treated his close friends quite well.

The day Dick returned from LA, Harry took him out and bought him a new Corvette as a token of his appreciation.

The two weeks went by very fast and before they knew it, Dick and Harry were in Hollywood. They were staying in one of the Studio's apartments. They were very nice accommodations. Dick had driven the Corvette out there, so they had transportation at their disposal.

They began shooting the picture the Monday after Harry flew in.

Dick had some free time on his hands, and he chose not to go to the filming. It wasn't long before he met Laura…

Chapter Six

The shooting of the film was going just top rate. The studio was delighted to find that Harry was a quick study and showed up on time with all of his lines learned.

Dick was very much concerned in the beginning about Harry's discipline. It wasn't that Harry didn't have a work ethic. He did. It was just that he had a bigger party ethic and sometimes that got the best of his work ethic. It was not the case on the *Twenty-eight Hours* set. Harry showed up on the set every morning with a game face on. He brought the same intensity to his newly discovered talent for acting as he brought to his singing.

Dick decided to stay at home this particular morning. It was a perfect Los Angeles day. It was warm with a bright sun shining down and the ever-present LA breezes had blown the smog out to sea.

He was having Eggs Benedict on the veranda of the small cottage that Fortune Studios had provided. They also provided room service and maid service and Dick was just enjoying the morning. He was marveling at the good fortune that he and Harry had been blessed with. He thought how different it was from the windy, snowy Chicago he had left not too long ago.

It was in this euphoric state of mind that brand new attorney, Richard Stuart, was thunderstruck. On the veranda of the adjoining cottage stood the most beautiful woman Dick Stuart had ever seen. She was blonde with blue eyes. She was fairly tall, but not so tall that Dick didn't stand over her.

She had obviously just stepped from the shower. She was wearing shower sandals on her feet and a terry cloth bathrobe. Dick couldn't help but wonder if she had anything on under that robe. The thought made his pulse quicken. She must have worn a shower cap because she still had droplets of water on her face and on that part of her chest that wasn't covered by the robe. She was brushing out a long, magnificent head of beautiful blonde hair. She was fully concentrating on the brushing of her hair. When she was done, she tossed her head making her hair flow with all its beauty. It made Dick gasp.

She looked up and saw Dick watching her. She was somewhat startled at Dick's presence for she wasn't aware that she wasn't quite alone. She immediately flashed the most gorgeous smile Dick had ever seen. "Hi," she said.

Dick was in love. That fast and that hopelessly. He had been watching her with a forkful of Eggs Benedict halfway raised to his mouth.

"Are you gonna eat those eggs or are you gonna just hold them there like that?" she said with what Dick would later call her "impish grin."

Dick finally pulled himself together and found his manners. "I'm sorry," he said. "I didn't mean to stare, but you are the most beautiful woman I have ever seen."

He had just embarrassed himself. It wasn't his way to be so forthcoming, but he was afraid that if he didn't act quickly she might disappear.

"Well, thank you," she said, "I hope Fortune Studios agrees with you."

"Fortune Studios?" asked Dick. "Are you working for them?"

"Well," she said, "I guess so. I took a screen test about four weeks ago and so far all I've gotten is some "extra" work on the set of that movie they're shooting with Harry Foster." She added,

"I think that's going to be a big hit. That Harry Foster can act pretty good for a lounge singer," she said.

Dick started to laugh.

"Why are you laughing? Don't you think Harry Foster can act?"

"I certainly do," returned Dick. "I'm his agent and lawyer." Then they both laughed.

"Would you care to join me for breakfast?" Dick finally asked.

She looked at him for a minute. *I probably shouldn't*, she thought, *but there is something about this man. He's here in the city, but he sure feels country to me.*

"My name is Dick Stuart. And yours?"

She made her decision. "Laura. Laura McNanty. Scottish through and through I am, and I would love to join you for breakfast. I am starved!"

This was how it happened. This is how two people fell in love over a breakfast of Eggs Benedict. Before the morning meal was over they had touched each other more deeply than any others had ever been able to. They found that they both had country backgrounds. They were both from south of the Mason Dixon line and they both thought the other was wonderful. Dick Stuart and Laura McNanty were lovers and in love. They were both happier than either had ever been.

With the schedules they both kept, finding time together was very difficult. It was a sandwich here, a quick cocktail there, and quick love-making whenever possible. It was always wonderful. The first time she touched him it was wonderful and it was no different the next time. He always marveled at how new it always seemed. He could never get enough of her. A weaker relationship would have failed.

They had managed to steal a whole day and night and decided that the water was the place they wanted to spend this one night of nights. They were in a secluded harbor aboard the boat of their dreams. It was fifty-five feet long and had a master sleeping quarters only seen in yachting magazines. The galley was stocked with food to last for days and the onboard bar was filled with fine wines and exotic cordials. Outside the portholes the view was breathtaking. They could see white sand and palm trees. The waves lapped against the shore with muted persistence and the sky was starting to give into the night. It was magnificent.

They had just had a wonderful meal of shellfish and white wine. They had taken turns sipping, laughing, and feeding one another bits of lobster and scallops, and snow-white crabmeat. These tasty morsels were dipped in a sauce as delicate as the blinking of the gathering stars. The two were in heaven.

She was wearing the bottom of her bathing suit and an old t-shirt on top. To him it seemed as though it were an ensemble from Rodeo Drive. The t-shirt was printed with the logo from the film Harry had been shooting. It was a large clock that had twenty-eight hours on it. Dick still thought the title was cheesy, but on her it was a thing of beauty.

The sky had turned deep blue. It was almost black. It was embossed with a million stars that looked to be a blanket of diamonds just blinking back at them. They had gone topside to enjoy another bottle of wine, the beautiful sky, and each other. The wine was a soft Merlot and she had cut up bits of cheese and a crusty loaf of French bread. It was a night especially made for lovers. They had gone forward on the boat where he had earlier placed soft cushions on the deck. They were lying down facing each other just nibbling on one another's lips with soft kisses. She sat up to pour them another glass of wine and the soft warm breeze of the night brushed across her t-shirt. It made her nipples hard. He loved that about her. He reached up and lightly rubbed the hardened nipple with the back of his hand. Her eyes glistened and she quickly removed the t-shirt. It made his pulse quicken to gaze upon her nakedness. He sat up on one elbow and took one of her nipples in his mouth and rolled his tongue around it while sucking gently. It made her let out a slight gasp of pleasure. He loved that about her, too. She was not too shy to let him know that she was feeling pleasure. It made him hard. He kissed from nipple to nipple until he had kissed them back to softness. He moved his head up to kiss her neck right where it met her shoulder. It gave her a chill and made her nipples hard again. He loved it.

He reached between her legs and, with her help, removed the bottom of her bathing suit. He reached for her and found her to be as wet as the waves crashing on the shore. With his hands he pleasured her. He was deep inside of her at one moment and then caressing that spot that felt so good. His hands were strong and he loved to pleasure her this way. She began to arch her back from the pleasure of it and reached down to hold him in her hands. Her touch was electric. They both removed his bathing suit.

When she took him in her hand she was pleased to see that he was as wet as she. She then bent over and took him in her mouth. She rolled her tongue all around him and especially underneath where it made him groan with pleasure. She was gentle, but insistent and it was driving him to that place where only she could take him. He wasn't quite ready to go there. He pulled her head up and kissed her deeply. He found the taste of her mouth and his taste in her mouth to be a sensual pleasure like few others. He laid her back and began to kiss her all along her belly until he came to the v of her legs. He could smell her sensuality and wanted more than anything to taste it. He put his tongue deep inside of her and she let out a little cry of pleasure. He reached up to kiss her and the mixture of feminine and masculine tastes was an absolute aphrodisiac. He wanted this to never end.   He moved his head back down to her wetness and began kissing and licking and loving the taste of her again. He just couldn't get enough of it. She began to writhe and call his name. There was nothing else in her world right now, but these feelings and that mouth that felt so wonderful and it made her come as though she were going to die. She trembled and closed her eyes and she was off into the million star sky that was above them.

He moved back up to her face and kissed her deeply. He always loved to make her come first and this time was no exception. He knew that the rewards for his giving pleasure would be receiving pleasure such as no other had ever been able to give him. This night would be no exception. She reached for him again. She found him to be soaking wet and that made her smile. She loved that she could do that to him. She slowly rubbed him up and down and it caused him to shiver just as she had done. When she felt that he might be nearing a climax she stopped and began to kiss his mouth deeply and with great hunger. It was with that same hunger that she took him once again into her mouth. She moved her head up and down until the moisture of her mouth and the moisture on him were one and the same. She lifted her head and kissed him deeply; she, too, enjoying the mixture of tastes that their lovemaking had produced.

It also had started those feelings deep in her stomach all over again. She straddled him and began rubbing the head of his cock on her nipples. It made him groan again and she loved it. She then sat over him and began to rub him on that spot between her legs that felt so good. She lifted up and put him deep inside of her and began to slowly move up and down and back and forth. That caused his cock to rub against her clit and she felt that wonderful feeling building again. It was building to another climax that she knew would feel even better than the first. He waited until she began to come and then gave up to the feelings he could no longer resist. She leaned over and kissed him deeply while they both came. He filled her and she drew every drop of him into her. She didn't stop until every bit was gone and she had it all. He had to beg her to stop.

This was the night of nights. It was the night that Dick asked Laura to marry him. It was also the night that Dick's world crashed around his ears.

Laura's eyes clouded with palpable sadness. "I can't," she said. "I've worked too hard and I'm too close to making my career finally work out. I love you, Dick, I really do. I can't take time out for marriage right now."

Chapter Seven

Dick had a good view of the stage. He was so close he could see the design on the Commissioner's tie. It was the opening round of the 1978 IFL draft and Dick, as always, was excited. He had started his sports agency three years prior and had built it to where it was today, a highly lucrative enterprise. He had finally gotten past Laura and her shocking rejection of his marriage proposal. He knew that there would never be another like her, but it probably was for the best. She was in love with her career and it would never have lasted. Harry was in the middle of another film, a sequel to his first one, which ended up being titled *A Star So Bright*. It was quite successful and launched his career to the next level. He spoke to Harry on occasion, but seldom saw him, as they lived on opposite coasts. Dick had made his home in Savannah and Harry moved to LA. Harry was getting the reputation as a heavy drinker with, at times, quite raucous behavior, but he had gone on to be a brilliant entertainer despite all of this baggage. Dick had felt for a long time that he needed a strong woman to settle him down, however, Harry loved ALL women and had no interest in just one of them.

The Stuart Agency had done well for itself on draft day. Seven of its clients had gone in the first two rounds. This would translate into strong commissions for the business. On numerous occasions he thanked his lucky stars he'd had the foresight to go in this career direction, rather than the path of corporate law. It was a natural for him. He always had a love of sports and the demand for attorneys in the sport agent business had grown dramatically in recent years.

He could have easily stayed on with Harry as his lead counsel, but couldn't stand it due to the close proximity to Laura, so he ran as far away as he could get.

He settled on Savannah for several reasons, the chief of which was the fact it that the city was off the beaten path. With his remuneration from Harry's first contract, he was able to build a charming bungalow on the Savannah River. It certainly wasn't opulent, but was very uniquely designed with lots of stained glass. Shortly after moving in, Dick purchased a twenty-foot Aquasport with twin 135's that could reach the ocean in less than thirty minutes. The ocean was the place that allowed Dick to completely unwind. He now had eight employees at the agency, and they were competent enough to run it while he was gone. He wasn't rich, but Dick was very, very comfortable and on his way…he had found his niche.

Meanwhile, Harry was in the middle of his second movie called *The Second Coming of Fame,* more or less a continuation of the life of Freddie Quick, the fictitious Rock and Roll star he portrayed in *A Star.* Part of the movie was to be filmed in Las Vegas, where "Freddie" would be performing at a popular casino. They had just wrapped the shoot at the studio and were preparing to move all operations to Las Vegas to finish the movie. Harry had three or four days off so he decided to visit his east coast friend.

Dick had just returned from New York, and had gotten the staff moving on ten new pro football contracts. Beginning next week, the real work would start, but meanwhile, it was time to play. He had just arrived at home, kicked off his shoes, and was mixing a drink when the call came.

"Hey! asshole! You gonna come and get me or not?"

Dick knew at once it was Harry and replied, "Where in the hell are you?"

"At this sorry excuse for an airport you've got," Harry retorted.

Same ol' Harry, Dick thought. "Stay there. I'll be there in twenty-five minutes."

When he got to the airport, Dick didn't see Harry anywhere. The Savannah Airport wasn't that large. Dick became concerned when at first he didn't spot his friend. He headed toward the customer service desk but was stopped by a rabbi who said, "Dick…it's me…Harry." Dick was astonished, not only by the realistic disguise, but also by the two goons standing on either side of Harry.

"Harry…what the…"

"I'll explain on the way to your place," Harry interrupted. The four men piled into Dick's Mercedes. There was little room to spare, given the size of the two goons.

"Sorry, pal. I have to travel like this all the time now— otherwise, I'd get mobbed," Harry explained. "That's why I have these two guys with me. I gotta have protection from all of my adoring fans."

"Oh, brother," groaned Dick

"Hope you have some extra room," Harry said.

"No problem," Dick advised, and wondered to himself how Harry could live like he did. When they reached the bungalow, they proceeded to catch up and get drunk, not necessarily in that order.

Dick gunned the engines on his boat and quickly trimmed it out. He headed toward the ocean to take Harry fishing. Harry used to tell him in their Army days how much he liked to fish off the coast of Massachusetts.

"Well, Harry," Dick explained in a shouting voice, "we'll be fishing for Cobia today. If we get lucky, we could get one fifty pounds plus!"

When they reached the big water, Dick got up in the tower while Harry put on a live Cigar minnow and eased the boat forward. In about ten minutes, Dick spotted the telltale fin of the Cobia, feeding in about five feet of water.

He shouted at Harry, "Shut it down, then cast in the direction of the big fish."

Harry held his breath as the quarry took the bait and started running with it. "Holy shit," Harry yelled as he set the hook on the monster.

Dick got a good look at her and shouted down to Harry, "Hang on, baby! She'll go at least sixty pounds!"

Later that night after they had feasted, Harry would say that the trip he took today ranked right up there with the all-time best. Then it became quiet as they gazed at the cozy fire Dick had kindled earlier.

"Harry, are you happy? I mean really happy?" Dick asked.

Harry thought for a while and then said, "I'm looking for something, Dick...dunno what it is...but I just can't find it."

There was a long silence before Dick finally said, "I think I know what it is."

"What?" Harry asked.

"It's peace, Harry. You're looking for peace," Dick told him.

The fire grew dim and Harry had fallen asleep in front of it. Dick got a blanket to throw over him, threw another log on the fire and left him on the floor in front of the glowing light. He trudged off to bed himself.

Chapter Eight

Harry lay in front of the fire awake for quite a while. He had the most disquieting feeling that had awakened him from a dead sleep. It kept him awake for most of the night. He was thinking about the past few years. He thought about how successful both he and Dick were. He thought about the possessions that they both had and he wondered if Dick was happy and he knew that he was not.

Dick always seemed happier than Harry, but maybe that was because he always seemed to know exactly where he was going. Harry always had another show, another film, another tour, but Dick was always grounded. He always seemed to have everything under control.

He decided that he would get up and take a drive. He didn't think that Dick would mind if he borrowed the car. He just couldn't get to sleep and taking a drive to the coast might help.

He decided to drive down to the Savannah River. It always cleared his head to walk in the fog. It had been true since he was a kid in Boston. He used to drive over to Revere Beach and just walk along the sea wall. He always loved how quiet the world became when it was wrapped in fog.

He was just leaving the house when one of his bodyguards stopped him and said, "Goin' out, boss?"

"Yeah," answered Harry.

The bodyguard rubbed his eyes and sleepily asked, "You want I should go with you, boss?"

"Nah," said Harry. "It's late and there's no reason why you can't get some sleep. Just goin' for a drive down by the river or maybe to the coast. I won't be long," he added.

Harry jumped into the Mercedes, clicked the button on the garage opener, and started the motor. He was impressed at how comfortable the car was. Harry was a sports car guy, but this big Mercedes sedan was awfully comfortable. He slowly backed the car out of the driveway and into the street.

He found Route 170 that he knew crossed the river. He traveled for a while until he came to the Savannah River. He found a place to park the Mercedes and got out to take a walk. It was three a.m. He didn't pay any attention to how long he walked. He just walked and enjoyed the fog and cool night air.

He thought he had a great idea. He was going to suggest that Dick and he do one more road trip. Start in Georgia and not stop until they reached California. They could both afford it now and it certainly would be a hoot. It would be just the two of them. No phones, no clients, no shows, no nothin'; just two best friends on an adventure. They were in their mid-thirties now and it was time to get on with it.

As he approached the car, he saw two men trying to force their way into the beautiful luxury sedan. He started running towards the car shouting,   "Hey! What are you doin' over there? Get away from that car!"

They turned to face him. One of the men had a ring of keys that must have held 200 car keys of every description. He was in the process of trying to find the right key for Dick's car. The other man had a crow bar in his hand. The crow bar was just in case none of the keys fit this car they were currently trying to steal. They were both dressed all in black and they weren't about to take any guff from Harry. They were going to steal this car and that was all there was to that.

The one with the keys was a skinny little weasel type of a guy, but the one with the crowbar was a pretty hefty size. The weasel kept working while the big guy started towards Harry.

"What the fuck do you want, asshole?" demanded the big guy. The weasel started to giggle and kept working on the door lock.

"That's my buddy's car," said Harry. "You can't fuck with that car," he added.

"Oh, I can't?" said big guy. "Did ya hear that, mate?" big guy said to the weasel.

"Yeah, I heard that," answered the weasel. He started to giggle even louder.

"Why is that?" said big guy.

"Because I'm not gonna let you," answered Harry. That set the weasel off into a convulsion of giggles.

"He's not gonna let us. Oh, God, that's funny," said the weasel.

"Really?" said the big guy. "How you gonna stop us"?

"I'll kick your ass," said Harry.

Harry no sooner got the words out when the crow bar started towards his head. Harry was ready. He sidestepped the blow and put a well-placed kick to the big guy's groin. It happened so fast that Harry's aim was just a bit off and the kick failed to put the big guy to the ground. It infuriated the big guy. He had dropped the crow bar, but came up bellowing with a backhand swing that caught Harry just above the temple. It stunned him and knocked him backwards. He was amazed at how quickly this big guy could move. The big guy tackled Harry and they both went down in a heap. Harry was being pummeled with fists and he was beginning to lose consciousness. Harry knew that if he went out, he would probably be killed. He decided not to die that day. He drove the heel of his hand as hard as he could against the big guy's nose. The brute blinked in amazement, looked at Harry, and then collapsed on him. He was dead. Harry had driven the cartilage of the big guy's nose into his brain.

The weasel looked at the big friend and then at Harry and said, "Holy shit…you fuckin' killed him…I don't believe it!" Weasel ran away.

The next thing Harry was aware of was police cars and sirens and ambulances. He was in one of the police cars and he was handcuffed. He listened to a seedy looking, overweight sheriff saying, "You have the right to remain silent."

"Hold it, hold it," said Harry. "What are you doin? Why aren't you arresting that skinny little prick?" demanded Harry.

"What skinny little prick would that be, mister?" asked the sheriff. "You mean my nephew, Larry? Why would I do that? Why, he told me that you came running up to him and his friend—the one lying under that sheet deader 'n hell—hollering something about your car. They tried to explain that they were just out for a walk along the river when you did some kind of kung-fu or karate thing on his buddy and killed him. I think you ought to be listening to this here Miranda warning I'm givin' you," he added sarcastically.

They booked him, printed him, and gave him some dungarees to wear and said, "Okay, you get that one phone call now. Better make it a good one."

"Hello," said Dick, looking at the clock. 4:15 a.m.

"Dick, it's Harry. I'm in trouble…"

Chapter Nine

Harry watched intently as the rain streamed down the windows in the Day Room. He was almost in a trance, mesmerized by the steady downpour. He was alone. He was standing on the edge of a deep black vortex, trying frantically not to fall into the dark spiral. Suddenly there was a reprieve, a tap on his shoulder and a soft pleasant voice…

"Mr. Foster, it's time for your medicine."

Obediently Harry took the small cup of medication and swallowed with the assistance of a glass of water.

"Can I get you anything else, Mr. Foster?" the nurse asked.

Harry shook his head and resumed his fixation with the panes of glass awash with the drizzling rain. It had been six long months since Harry's trial, which ended in his acquittal. The damage to Harry was devastating and adversely affected others close to him, particularly, Dick. He had arranged for the best defense attorney money could buy and Dick, with no background in criminal law, was nonetheless quite effective as Harry's co-counsel.

As it turned out, Dick could have probably handled the case himself, given the bungling of the inept sheriff and his nephew, the weasel. The weasel had left several of his prints on the Mercedes near the lock and there were some small scratches around it as well. With this evidence and strong cross-examination of the weasel, he was caught like a rat in a trap. In addition, he incriminated his uncle, the sheriff of Sumter County, Ga.

Unfortunately, the scandal of the incident took its toll. Harry was unable to return to the shooting of his second film due to his bail stipulation. He was not allowed to leave the county.

The studio cancelled the film and filed suit against Harry for the breach of his contract plus the resulting large losses. Dick handled the suit on his behalf, but could do little more than to settle out of court for 90% of Fortune's net loss on the film. With the exception of Harry's residence in LA, the settlement wiped him out. Due to his extensive involvement with Harry's legal troubles, Dick was forced to sell his agency. He actually had to use some of the funds to help Harry. Dick felt it was his turn to support his friend. Like always, this was the way it was with these two.

Harry fell into deep depression and began to drink heavily. This soon led to drugs and Harry was broke. All of this self-abuse by Harry occurred despite living with Dick in his river house.

Dick could not be with Harry around the clock. Although Dick was handsomely paid for his business, he had to begin looking for other means of livelihood. This meant that he would be out of town frequently, sometimes days at a time. It was on one of these visits that Dick returned to find Harry unconscious on his couch. Dick, unable to revive him, called 911 immediately.

Harry had suffered a drug overdose, complicated by excessive alcohol consumption.

Harry recovered several days later and Dick picked him up from the hospital. As Dick was driving, he told Harry that he had to get some help or he was going to kill himself. Dick was surprised when Harry quickly agreed. This was how Harry came to be at The Glades.

The Glades was a multi-care clinic that treated substance abuse and several forms of mental illness. Harry was diagnosed with major depression accompanied by related alcohol and drug dependency.

He had been at this place for thirty days and had overcome, or at least had learned how to handle his urge for whiskey and downers, but he was in and out of depression. He seldom wanted to do anything. He looked forward to sleeping in the dark and always wanted to be alone. He would sleep for twenty-four hours if they would let him. It was fortunate for Harry that the staff of The Glades would not permit him to sleep or spend time by himself with the exception of the seven hours allotted at night. He was to meet with a new psychologist today. It was to be a psychologist that would be with Harry for the duration of his stay at the Glades.

Dr. Amber Adkinson was a woman in her early thirties who had received her medical degree from Southern Methodist University in Dallas. She had been at the Glades for a year now and had gained the reputation as a highly competent and dedicated physician.

She was a stunning, auburn-haired beauty hidden behind a pair of ungainly spectacles. Harry was unaware that she was a big fan of his from the very beginnings of his career.

He entered her office and quietly sat down and waited patiently while she finished a paper on which she had been working.

"Hello, Mr. Foster. I'm Doctor Adkinson."

They talked for about a half an hour and, for the most part, it was a pleasant conversation. Toward the end of the session however, the doctor got right in his face and basically chewed his ass out like it hadn't been since his Army days. She told him she wanted him to read a book and thrust it in his hands. It was entitled *Fire in the Belly*.

Harry left her office and was tingling. No one had spoken to him like that in years! And when she took her glasses off and stared him in the eye…well, it just left him breathless. Harry was confused, but he was bound and determined to read the book, if for no other reason than to please her. He went to the Day Room and sat down next to a window. He didn't notice that it had stopped raining as he turned to page one. Harry stayed with the book until it was time for bed. After lights out, he turned on his little table lamp and stayed up past two a.m. until he finished it. He lay on his bed and before drifting off, he began to put the pieces of the puzzle together one at a time…

Chapter Ten

Harry awoke from his sleep at the outrageous hour of 7:30. It had been his custom to be awake all night and go to sleep at 7:30. He found it easier to deal with his situation if he slept while everyone else was awake, and was awake when everyone else was sleeping. This was the nature of his depression. So deep had it become that he didn't want to deal with anyone or anything. It was not unusual for very successful people to fall into this type of depression. People who are accustomed to being able to handle stressful situations, when faced with one they can't seem to handle, simply shutdown.

Harry had shut down. He had shut down almost totally. He didn't often shave. He rarely combed his hair. He would take a shower because the staff forced him to. He was just a shell of the Harry Foster that the rest of the world knew. This suited him just fine. Then he met Dr. Amber Adkinson. He also read the book she had given him. He made his decision on that night to start the slow process back from the living hell he had been in for the past six months that had culminated with his being placed at the Glades.

Dr. Amber Adkinson was upset with herself. She had gone too far with her patient. That her patient was Harry Foster Jr. made no difference. She knew better than to push a patient as hard as she had pushed Mr. Foster. She had sensed an inner strength in the man and wanted to tap into it. She had shown impatience and in the world of psychotherapy that was unacceptable. More damage could be done to a patient by rushing the therapy than almost any other error a psychologist could make. She knew this and did it anyway.

Dr. Amber Adkinson was a stunning beauty. She was tall, five foot seven, and trim. Her hair was a deep auburn red, so full and thick that both men and women just wanted to put their hands in it. Her figure was ample. Her legs long and lean, her waist very small, and her breasts were the envy of every other cheerleader at SMU and the desire of every man who met her. Her eyes were blue, but sometimes green, and other times gray. They seemed to pick up the surrounding colors and choose which looked best. Her skin was soft and smooth and her smile would make others smile and her laugh could light up a room. She was by anybody's standard, an absolute beauty.

She took extra care in dressing this morning. She wore a beautiful emerald green suit with an ivory colored silk blouse under the jacket. Her hair, rich and full, was shoulder length and wavy and looked wonderful against the green and ivory of her outfit. She applied make-up sparingly, but carefully. She decided against the pearls because, after all, she was going to work and not out to dinner. She decided on her contact lenses this morning instead of the glasses she normally wore. When she was finished, she stood in front of the full-length mirror in her hallway. She knew in her heart of hearts why she was dressing this way and she felt slightly guilty.

When she looked at the reflection coming back at her, she said, "Well, Mr. Harry Foster Junior, I'll bet this helps your depression. It's certainly making me feel pretty good," she added.

When he walked into her office she looked up and was startled. Harry Foster Jr. was shaven, combed, and dressed. He looked like the actor she had seen on the silver screen. Yesterday he looked like a thousand patients she had seen before. He was disheveled and completely disengaged from life.

"I read the book," he stated. "I read it all last night."

She looked back at him and said, "Really, Mr. Foster, do you want to talk about it? What did you think of it?"

"Well, at first the guy in the book pissed me off. Oh, excuse me, Doc. I didn't mean to be disrespectful," he added quickly.

"That's quite alright, Mr. Foster," she said. "Go on."

"Well, like I said, the guy pissed me off at first, but then I started feeling badly for him. You know, all this whiney bullshit about poor me, woe is me, yada, yada, yada."

He went on to say, "Then I realized he was talking about all of the same feelings that I've been having. I haven't cared about anything or anybody but myself for the past six months. I've been taking advantage of the people around me and, he added, I've been taking advantage of the best friend I have in the world. Dick Stuart has given up just about everything he has to help me. I've been lying around here feeling sorry for myself for a month; not to mention the five or six months prior to coming here that I was so drunk or so stoned I hardly remember them.

"I was lying in my bed last night and I got to thinking, 'Hey, Foster…what are you doin'? You can't lie up in bed like this anymore! Get off your ass! You're Harry Foster Jr. You're better than that. You're Enrico Fastallo Jr.

"The way you hollered at me yesterday, Doc. Nobody has dared to holler at me like that for a long time." He then added, "Look, Doc, if I can make a beautiful woman like you angry enough to holler at me, then I'm doing something wrong. I've got to straighten my act out. I know that I have a long way to go. Doc, will you help me?"

Amber flushed when he said she was beautiful. It gave her a warm rush as if something were humming inside her stomach. She tried to fight this feeling and knew that professionally she should pass this patient off. She tried, but failed. "Of course I will, Mr. Foster."

"Do you think you could call me Harry, Doc?"

Chapter Eleven

The auctioneer's gavel fell for the last time. Dick watched as the successful bidders began to load his possessions in their respective vehicles…lock, stock, and barrel, it was all gone. He had sold his river front home two weeks ago and all that was left was to pack his clothes in the luggage and then load it into the Mercedes.

He had seldom run from anything in his life, but felt it was time to leave all his problems associated with his time in Savannah behind. He had no idea what he was going to do, with the exception of a short trip down to Sebring, Florida, to visit his friend Harry at the clinic there. Harry had been there for eight weeks and only now was allowed to have visitors other than immediate family. Like Harry, Dick had no family, another incredible bit of circumstance that locked them together for the past fifteen years. Money was not a problem for Dick, despite the outlay of cash he had used to help Harry. He had done well on the sale of his business, home, and all his possessions. Dick knew one other thing—he was through being a lawyer.

He left the following morning and made the six-hour drive to The Glades.

He was startled when he saw his friend. He looked marvelous—fit and trim and at least five years younger.

"Well," Dick said, "this place certainly agrees with you!"

Harry embraced him and kissed his cheek in top Italian fashion and was crying as he choked, "I've been to hell, buddy, but I'm back. God damn it, I'm back!"

Nothing more was said as they sat down and Dick waited for Harry to re-gain his composure.

Harry then related most of what had gone on for the past two months and Dick was proud of what Harry had accomplished. He had lost his appetite for booze and pills and there was something of a glow about his persona. Dick was just amazed.

Dick proceeded to tell Harry what he had just done in the past two weeks and that he was giving up law.

Tears welled in Harry's eyes again and Dick regretted he'd said anything about it.

"Dick," Harry said fighting for control of his emotions, "I'm sorry. I feel like a piece of shit for what I've put you through. Now you're giving up the most important thing in your life and it's my fault."

"No, no, my friend. You had nothing to do with it," Dick replied. "I'm burned out. I need to do something else with my life."

Harry said, "Dick, I swear to you, I will pay you back for everything you've done, if it's the last thing I do."

"Your debt was paid a long time ago, amigo. Had it not been for you, I wouldn't have a million bucks in the bank right now and the freedom to do whatever the fuck I want to," Dick explained. "And if there's anything else you need, just let me know and I'll get it."

"No," Harry said. "I'll be fine…I put my house for sale last month and have already received two offers. I think I'm going ahead and get rid of it."

"What are you going to do, Harry?" Dick asked.

"I've been doing some serious thinking since I've been here, Dick. You were right on that night when you said you knew what I was looking for. It WAS peace, just as you said," Harry advised, "and I believe I've found it."

"That's great, Harry. If anybody deserves it, it's you," Dick remarked. "Why don't you tell me about it."

"Part of it has to do with what I'd like to try after I get out of here," Harry said. "I want to go back to what I did when I started my career in Chicago. Acoustical music, real music, not the kind of crap they're putting out today. Maybe a restaurant or supper club to go with it," Harry stated.

"Sounds like fun, Harry," Dick volunteered. "Have you thought about where?"

"Not really...but I plan to soon," Harry answered. "And there's something else, Dick. I want you involved with me as a full partner."

"Tell you what, buddy," Dick replied. "You let me mull that one over a while and I'll let you know. However, right now, I think I'm going to head down to Key West since I'm this far south, and do some serious Bonefish angling. I've always wanted to try it."

Dick went on, "You're getting discharged on the fourteenth, right?"

Harry nodded and Dick continued, "So, I'll be back next week to get you and we'll talk more. Okay?"

As Dick turned to leave, Harry grabbed his sleeve and said, "Wait, Dick. There's one more thing. It has to do with how I was led to my peace." He paused.

"Oh, hell," he said. "Go on your trip and I'll tell you when you get back."

Chapter Twelve

Dick was in the Jon boat. He was having a wonderful time. *This Bonefish is one crafty devil to catch,* he thought to himself.

His guide, a tall and lanky black man named David was expertly putting him where he needed to be to hook on but it wasn't easy. He would feel a lightning strike and then the fish would be gone. He just couldn't quite get it right.

David said with a slight accent of Jamaica, "C'mon, boss, you can do it. You have to be a little patient and wait to set the hook, you know? If you wait but a moment you'll hook him just fine. Then you'll know what a game fish is like," he said in the lyrical tones of the islands. His instructions sounded almost musical.

David saw, from his poling perch, another group of Bonefish and started to quietly pole over to them.

"Remember, boss, wait for but a moment for the silver devil to take the hook and then lift the rod tip straight up," said the ebony guide. "Then you'll be holdin' on," he added.

Dick felt the tug on his line. He waited. He felt the fish take off with the fly David had put on the line. He waited. He felt the fish take a sharp turn to the left and he lifted his rod tip. The absolute bending of his fly rod rewarded him. That fish almost tugged it out of his hands and bent the tip all the way down to the water.

"Ooh, whee!" exclaimed David. "You got him now, don't ya see?"

Dick was amazed at the strength of this fish. He knew that they weren't all that big and the power of the thing took him by surprise. He was an expert fisherman and never for a moment did he lose control of the situation. When he finally landed the fish, he was elated.

David hopped down from his perch, reached into the water, and with his bony black hand, expertly pulled the silver fish from the water. "It's a fine fish you have there, boss," he praised. "You did a fine job also bringin' him in and all," he added.

Dick was happy. He looked around as David unhooked the fish. He could see the Keys from the boat. He knew that if he turned about and could see far enough north, he would be able to see the Everglades and as he looked to the east, he could see the open ocean. He watched this magnificent black man working with absolute expertise and he thought of his own background.

My God, he thought, *look at all the different realms of the world I can see and feel just from this one vantage point...*

Dr. Amber Adkinson was at home. She was in the Jacuzzi tub up to her neck. The water was bubbling about and she was troubled.

Tomorrow was the day that Harry Foster was leaving. He had made a remarkable turnaround in only eight weeks. She knew it had more to do with the strong will of Harry than any of her counseling, but that was not what was troubling her. She was troubled by the feelings she had developed for Harry over the past two months. She liked the feelings, but she knew they were totally unprofessional. It was common for patients to fall in love with their therapists. In fact, one of the indications that the patient was getting well was that they were no longer in love with their therapist. It was uncommon for a therapist to fall in love with a patient. This was an uncommon moment in Amber's life...she had, in fact, fallen in love with one of her patients. She had tried to tell herself that it was because of his celebrity, but she knew better. She had listened to his life's story and listened to what he believed in and she knew that she loved him. She loved how he thought, his undying loyalty to those he loved, and maybe most of all, his sense of humor. She found herself laughing more than she should during her sessions with him. She tried to control herself but couldn't. She knew she could never confess her feelings to Harry.

She lay back in the Jacuzzi with thoughts of Harry Foster Jr. and that insistent hum deep in her belly started up again…

Harry was in his room at The Glades. He was leaving tomorrow and he had mixed feelings about it. He knew he wanted to get out of this place, but he was going to miss seeing the beautiful Dr. Amber Adkinson every day. He knew he was being foolish. *She's your God-damned doctor, you shit-head!* He thought to himself, *What the hell does she want with a washed up singer-actor?* Harry was also smart enough to realize that patients sometimes fall in love with their therapists. He was also smart enough to realize that this was not one of those times. He really had fallen in love with Dr. Amber Adkinson, who just happened to be his therapist. He thought to himself, *What makes you think that a beautiful, smart, and educated woman like Dr. Adkinson would even consider getting involved with a nut case like you?*

He lay back in his bunk with thoughts of Dr. Adkinson and that insistent hum deep in his belly started up again…

Dick was waiting in the lobby when Harry finally cleared the billing department. Harry was not surprised to see that the bill had already been taken care of by Dick. He came down and hugged Dick and said, "What the fuck did you pay the bill for?"

"Will you shudupp!" said Dick. "Let's get you the hell outta here."

"Wait a minute, Dick," said Harry. "I want you to meet somebody."

He went over to where Dr. Adkinson was talking to some other doctors and took her by the arm. "Dr. Amber Adkinson, I'd like you to meet Dick Stuart. He's the best friend I have in the world and I wanted him to meet the person who saved my life."

"I hardly saved your life, Mr. Foster," she said with a strange look on her face. The look was lost on Harry, but not on Dick. It made him smile.

"Excuse me for a moment, Dick," said Harry.

He took Dr. Adkinson by the elbow and moved her over to where the Florida sun came through the windows in the lobby of the Glades. "Listen, Doc," he said hesitantly. "I am truly grateful to you. I don't think I could have made it without your help. If there is ever anything I can do to help you, please call me."

He then added, "It would be my pleasure to do anything at all for you." He took both her hands in his and lightly kissed on her cheek. He kissed her in such a way that the corner of his mouth just touched the corner of hers. He stepped back, but still held her hands in his. He just looked into her eyes and then smiled. She turned and walked away.

She battled with her emotions as she walked away. *Tell him, you idiot!* she warred with herself. *You can't,* she fought back with herself. *You know you can't!*

That insistent hum started in her belly again. "Oh, God," she said...

As Harry watched her back, he too, fought within himself as she walked away. *Go get her, you knucklehead!* his inner voice screamed. *Yeah, she wants you. What...are you still nuts?"* That insistent hum started in his belly again. "Oh, God," he said...

"How you feelin', partner?" asked Dick.

"Just fine, just fine," Harry said and then stopped cold. "Whaddya mean, partner?" he asked.

"I mean, *partner*," said Dick. "I thought about your idea of going into business together and the more I thought of it, the more I like it," Dick added.

"I got an idea. I think your idea of opening a supper club is a great one," Dick said. He then said, "and I have the theme."

He went on to tell him about the bonefish trip he was on and how at one moment he could look out from the boat and see civilization in the vision of the Keys, he could see wild land in the vision of the Everglades, he could see other societies in the vision of the Jamaican guide, and he could see adventure in the vision of the open sea.

"I think we should open up a multiple room supper club. Each room would have its own theme. The menu would be different, the music would have the sound of the country or region it represented, and the wait staff would be all decked out in the uniform of the area they were representing. If a customer didn't like one room, he could go to another room or another 'realm.' I think that should be the name of it—Another Realm..."

Chapter Thirteen

"Harry! Harry!" "You didn't hear a damned thing I was saying, did you?" Dick asked, as they motored down the freeway.

"I'm sorry, Dick. I got something on my mind," Harry replied.

"Wanna talk about it?" Dick quizzed.

"Yeah, Dick…I do," Harry said.

He spent the next half an hour telling Dick about his feelings for Amber and how he felt that she was the one responsible for his self discovery and subsequent "peace." He related that he had never met a woman who had such a pull on his heart. She wasn't like any of the other women in his life. She never once threw herself at him. It was as if they met at some other level. It was a level that he had never experienced with another woman before. He went on and on, and it was obvious to Dick that Harry was deeply in love with this woman. He pulled the big Mercedes over and, with the engine idling, sat there in dead silence.

"Dick…what are you doing? Why have we stopped?" Harry asked.

"We're going back, Harry. I'm taking you back to her," Dick replied in a determined voice.

Over Harry's feeble objections, Dick rolled up to The Glades and killed the engine. He turned to Harry and said, "Get your bag and get your ass in there and resolve this situation right now. If you aren't back in ten minutes, and I hope you won't be, I'll be in Miami at the Flamingo Hotel," Dick concluded.

Harry got out, retrieved his suitcase and sheepishly waved goodbye to Dick.

As Harry entered the front door, Dick thought to himself, *There's two good reasons I'm doing this. One, Harry wouldn't be worth a shit to me as a business partner until this is resolved and, two, this is truly an affair of the heart, from which I doubt Harry will ever return.* He was still thinking this as he wheeled the big black sedan out of the parking lot and headed south.

Harry put his suitcase in the foyer and went directly to her office. He rapped lightly at the door and heard her say, "Come in."

When he opened the door and saw her, their eyes locked so intently that Harry failed to notice she'd been crying. In an instant, she was out from behind her desk and embraced tightly in his arms. There was no seduction, no moments of youthful innocence, and no words. It was groping, wild kissing, and writhing on her sofa. It was undeniable, uncontrolled passion. When it was over, Harry felt ashamed that he had somehow cheapened her, not to mention putting her career at great risk.

"I'm terribly sorry this happened, Amber," Harry said.

She put her forefinger to his lips and whispered, "Sshh...I love you."

That was all Harry needed. She had applied the "coup de grace" and he was reeling.

"I want to marry you, Amber," he said, not believing this was all happening.

"Let me take you home with me, Harry," in the most beautiful voice he'd ever heard.

Several days later, Dick was soaking up some rays on Miami Beach when his cell phone rang.

"Dick. It's me."

"I figured that, lover boy," Dick said chuckling.

"Don't get cute or I won't ask you to be my best man, asshole," Harry replied.

"Whaaat!?" Dick asked incredulously.

"We're getting married in three weeks and I want you to stand up for me, Dick."

Dick was somewhat stunned. Harry had changed so much in just a couple of months. He was humble, kind, and at peace.

"What a woman she must be, Harry. Of course I'll be your best man," Dick replied.

Harry said, "Why don't you come back up here to Sebring and check into a motel. It'll give you a chance to really get to know Amber and we'll fill you in on our wedding plans."

The wedding was to take place on the coming Saturday at a small chapel on the outskirts of the city. Dick had been around Harry and Amber for a couple of weeks, and was extremely impressed with the bride-to-be. They had been out to dinner a few times and Dick had visited Amber's tasteful condominium. She was an excellent cook and a most gracious host. Harry was completely infatuated with her. He doted after her and her wish was Harry's command.

Dick still had trouble believing that this was his old friend. On that Wednesday, Amber left for Orlando to pick up the wedding dress that she had purchased the week before. This gave Dick and Harry a chance to sit down together and discuss future business plans.

The meeting went fairly well, although Harry wasn't entirely focused on it. He seemed to like Dick's idea of club design, but he wasn't quite ready to give his final okay. It was finally decided that they would go to the Keys together, take a boat ride, and that might give Harry a better feel of what Dick was trying to convey.

They left Amber's condo and went out for a couple of drinks where they discussed the financials of the venture. They were heavily engrossed in discussion at a local lounge; so engrossed, that they failed to hear a news bulletin announced on the television at the bar. There had been a fiery accident on the freeway between Sebring and Orlando involving a tanker and a passenger vehicle. Harry would not learn of his Amber's tragic death until early the next morning...

Chapter Fourteen

It was more than he thought he could take. He had never loved any woman as he had loved Amber. She had made his world seem right. She had made his world right when it looked as though nothing could. She had saved him from a life of drug and alcohol abuse. She had made his life worth living again and now she was gone—completely gone.

All Harry had left of her was the engagement ring they took out of the ashes in the car and a photograph of Amber and himself standing in front of the car she was killed in. It wasn't much.

Since Amber had no family and Dick was the only family that Harry had, the funeral was a private affair. It was at a local funeral home with the services being held at St. Ann's Catholic Church in Sebring. It broke Harry's heart even further that he still didn't even know if she was Catholic, Protestant, or Jew. They hadn't known each other long enough to find out.

Harry had decided that the ashes would be strewn about the ocean. He decided on this because on one of the few evenings they had had together, she had said jokingly, "When I die, I want to be buried at sea." He felt in his heart that she actually meant that and was going to carry out her wish.

Harry had rented a fifty-foot Egg Harbor for the cruise out to sea. He wanted her to be at least fifty miles out. He didn't know why he chose fifty miles. He just did.

When Harry and Dick boarded the vessel the captain welcomed them both aboard. Harry didn't even acknowledge the captain. The captain knew his mission and the reasons surrounding the trip and just stood aside while Harry went forward. In both of his arms he held a beautiful urn. Harry was still struggling with the decision as to whether or not he would put the whole urn over the side or just spread his Amber's ashes on the water.

Harry stood on the forward deck with clenched jaws just staring out to sea. Dick stood off to the portside just watching his friend in his grief. He stood as a sentinel to guard Harry's privacy and to be close enough should Harry need him. It was all Dick could do and he felt helpless at his task.

The captain killed the engines. "Fifty miles, Mr. Foster," the captain said quietly.

Harry slowly began to open the urn. He had made his decision. He slowly spilled the contents of the urn over the deep blue waters. He watched as the ashes began to spread over the water and slowly begin to drop below the surface. Harry slowly reached into his pocket and produced the wedding band that Amber was to wear after they got married.

"I have loved you more than there are drops of water in this ocean, sweet Amber," Harry said. "With this ring, I thee wed," he said mournfully. He dropped the wedding band into the center of the now disappearing ashes on the water.

By this time, Dick had moved beside his friend. Harry turned to him with a look of despair that Dick had never seen on anyone before and said, "Man, what the fuck am I gonna do now?" He collapsed in tears in Dick's arms.

It had been a year and a half since Amber's death. Harry had completely immersed himself into the construction of Another

Realm. It was truly magnificent. It had the Tropical Room that would feature exotic birds and music of the Islands. It had the European Room that would change its featured country every night. One night would be Italy and the food and dress would be Italian. The next would be Germany and so on and so on. When reservations were made for this room, guests had no idea what country would be featured. The country was decided on the specific day by a lottery system.

A third room was the Circus Room with the accompanying accoutrements. The last room was the Amber Room.

This room was for special occasions and access could only be granted by Harry Foster. The colors of the room were soft and muted. They were yellows and browns and shades of amber. The seating was soft and plush and the centerpiece of the room was a beautiful urn set inside a small grotto that produced a small waterfall. The water that cascaded around this urn was salt water tapped right from the sea. The air had a slight aroma of Freesia. It was the scent that Amber wore. In the corner was a beautiful diamond engagement ring. The whole display was encased in glass. The room was named The Realm of Amber and Harry had complete control over what happened in this room.

This was Dick Stuart's vision and this was the vision that Harry carried out. It was a perfect partnership. Dick, with his legal abilities, could handle all the financials and Harry, with his people skills, could handle all the contractors.

It didn't hurt to pass the information that Harry Foster Jr. was in fact Enrico Fastallo Jr. if any contractor decided that he might like to get a little troublesome.

Uncle Antonio had reached out for Harry upon hearing of Amber's death and promised any service he could render. Many of these services were rendered without Harry's knowledge. It was because of these services that this enormous project was ready to go in a year and a half. It was an accomplishment that would have been impossible without the intervention of Uncle Antonio.

Opening night was star-studded. People from all over the country came to see the opening of Another Realm. The opening act was Harry and the Nomads, and people came from miles around to see the opening show.

All of Harry's friends from show business were there. All of Dick's associates from the legal world were there. And all of the people from Uncle Antonio's world were there.

Dick was in the dressing room with Harry. It was time to get dressed for the show and he and Dick were passing time.

"Harry," said Dick, "I just want you to know that I have been amazed at your resilience. I mean this 'Amber thing'."

Harry cut him off. "Look, Dick, it was Amber who taught me how to get through this stuff. If it weren't for her, I would be dead. I have to honor her memory by not failing."

Just then there was a knock on the door. Dick walked over to answer the door. He opened it. Standing in the doorway stood a vision from Dick Stuart's past—the screen star, Laura McNanty.

"Hi," she said. "Am I welcome?"

Chapter Fifteen

Dick just stood at the doorway speechless. Standing before him was the love of his life. He didn't know how to react. He didn't know if he should throw his arms around this woman or if he should throw this woman out. He had loved her with all his heart and she had broken it. She had been the author of the most painful memory in his life. It was a memory that could still evoke pain in his heart and could cause him to sink into a depression of monumental proportions.

He stepped aside and said, "Of course you are, Laura it's so nice to see you."

The nonchalance of the statement didn't fool Harry, it didn't fool Laura, and Dick certainly hadn't fooled himself. All three of them knew the apparent nonchalance of the moment was the only way Dick could handle this surprise.

Harry looked at Laura and said, "Oh, Laura, it is so good to see you. You look wonderful." She did, too. She was wearing a simple black evening dress that was set off by the appropriate jewelry. But it was neither the jewelry nor the beautiful dress that made her look so stunning. It was the healthy California tan she was sporting. It was the smile that had won Dick's heart so long ago, and it was her face, crowned by the magnificent, auburn hair that had become her trademark.

Many a man had fantasized about running his hands through that hair. It was still soft and luxurious, as Dick had remembered. It might even be more beautiful than Dick remembered it. Many a man had sat in a darkened theatre to watch Laura McNanty on screen and fantasized about making love with her. Dick never did. He never saw any of her movies. He just couldn't. It hurt too much.

A producer had spotted Laura in the cast of *A Star So Bright*. She wasn't on screen very long, but the scene had her in a wet t-shirt because Freddie Quick, the character that Harry played, had splashed her in a "drive by" splashing with his corvette. She was on screen for about ten seconds, but she was hard to miss. Those ten seconds took the breath away from millions of men across the country. The switchboard at Fortune Films lit up on the national release night of the film. There were thousands of phone calls from teen-aged boys and starry-eyed girls wanting to know who that woman in the t-shirt was.

Sig Libowitz, a producer who had been looking for a new star, took notice and reached out for Laura. He wanted to do an update of the film made famous by John Wayne and Maureen O'Hara called *The Quiet Man*. He had wanted to team her with Harry Foster, but Harry had declined. He said that his loyalty to Dick Stuart wouldn't allow for it. He didn't have any problem with Laura, but was afraid that Dick might resent it if he went to work with her.

The movie, named after the original, was a smashing success. It was a direct take from the old movie, to even include changing her once blonde hair to the wonderful auburn color that had become her trademark. With improvement in filming and scenery, the charm of the movie took the nation by storm. The people who saw the movie just loved it. It launched a career for Laura that included two Oscar nominations and three Golden Globe Awards.

She finally won her Oscar for her portrayal of a pill popping, insecure housewife who was married to a psychologically abusive husband in a film called *The Group*. She was called on to show her abilities as an actress through the complete spectrum of emotions. She laughed, she cried, she showed anger, and did it all with such believability that she won the Oscar that year, hands down, no competition.

When somebody came up to her after she had won and said, "Congratulations, Laura, this certainly is a night of nights for you!"

"Yes, it is," she managed to get out and smiled at her well-wisher. It was right after this she decided to go home.

She knew it wasn't really her "night of nights." Her thoughts went back to a beautiful boat and chilled shellfish. She thought of warm summer breezes and cold Chardonnay. She thought of two failed marriages and began to cry. She began to cry like a little girl. Her heart was broken because it had occurred to her that all of these awards meant nothing. All of this work and it meant nothing to her. The one thing that ever meant anything to her, she had walked away from.

She had read in the paper that Harry and Dick were opening a new club on the Keys of Florida. She was terrified, but she made the decision to go to opening night. She had to see Dick again and even though it would kill her if he didn't want to see her, she had to take the chance. She knew that every emotion she showed on the screen came from somewhere in her relationship with Dick Stuart. He was her definition of happiness. He was her definition of passion. He was her definition of heartbreak. He was her definition of what it meant to be alive and she knew that she still loved him and that she always would.

It was with great anticipation and fear that she booked a flight for Miami. The studio had offered to fly her in with the other dignitaries going to opening night of Another Realm. She had refused and had demanded a promise from all that they would not say anything to anybody that she was going.

She walked up to the giant who was covering the door at Another Realm.

"Hi," she said. "I'm Laura McNanty and I was wondering if it would be possible for me to see Dick Stuart?"

"I know who you are, Ms. McNanty," said the burly doorman. "You can do just about anything you want here, ma'am." He almost tripped over himself to get the door opened fast enough for Laura.

"Why, thank you so much," Laura said.

He walked her to the dressing room where he knew Dick and Harry were and said, "They're right in there, Ms. McNanty. Do you want I should knock on the door for you?" he asked.

"No, thank you," she said. "I'll take it from here." She stood in front of the door for a long pause. She took a deep breath and muttered, "Oh, God, please let him want to see me."

With that she knocked on the door. The door swung open and her heart stopped. The doorway was filled by Dick Stuart…

Chapter Sixteen

In the true fashion of "show business," the club called Another Realm had been shortened by the public to "The Realm" The public always wanted to turn the newest "hot spot" into a buzzword.

"Been to the Realm?"

"Goin' to the Realm?"

"I'm gonna meet her at the Realm." That's the way it was on the streets of the Florida Keys and it was only opening night.

Harry had just escaped the dressing room where he left Dick and Laura sort of staring at each other in the doorway. He just simply said, "I've got a show to do in five minutes...I gotta go." With that he just walked out the door leaving the two of them to figure it out.

The Nomads were already on stage. It was still Jocko Dunn on keyboards, Lou Bellino on bass, Dusty James on lead guitar, and out of retirement was Frank Lane on drums. He had retired last year, but this was one opening night he didn't want to miss. The band was situated right on stage in front of the curtain. The house lights went down. A white spotlight came on and was shining right on a spot just over Jocko's shoulder.

The band was already vamping and the announcer said from somewhere above the crowd, "Ladies and Gentleman, from the Amber Performance Center, and on behalf of Another Realm, we are proud to present...HARRY FOSTER JR!" The applause was deafening.

The boys opened with *That Long Lonesome Road,* and when they got through the first chorus, the curtains parted and revealed a twenty-six piece orchestra which included a six-piece string section. The music was magnificent and ended the song with a kick-ass big band arrangement worthy of either of the Dorsey Brothers' bands or Count Basie.

Harry was in his element.

As Harry looked out over the audience, he saw the entire gamut of society. He saw the world of Florida's political scene. People who just had to be seen here tonight.

He saw the world of "show business." People who just had to be seen here tonight.

He saw the very hip of Florida's social scene. People who just had to be seen here tonight.

He also saw the world of organized crime. People who were seen only when they wanted to be. The photographers who moved about the room were advised not to take any pictures of these people unless asked to. None of these people asked to have their picture taken.

Harry sang his heart out that night. He was the closest to happy he had been since losing Amber. Music could always do that to Harry. He had only one tough moment on stage when he sang a song that he and Jocko had written. It was done with just piano and bass. It was a boozy blues tune in the style of *One More For The Road* called *This One's for Amber.*

Harry sang it with everything he had in a single spotlight closed down just to light his face. All in the audience who knew about Amber were misty-eyed as well. The ending of the song brought a long moment of silence and then applause and finally ended with everyone in the room standing.

"I thank you for that, ladies and gentlemen," said Harry. And with a hitch in his voice said, "and Amber does, too."

"Ladies and gentlemen," said Harry. "In 1965, I met a man who would change the course of my life. I was a kid from Boston with an Italian background and a bit of a chip on my shoulder. I had just been drafted and I wasn't too happy to be in the army. I was lonely, didn't know anybody, and frankly didn't particularly trust anybody either. So, naturally," he went on, "I picked this emaciated, wisecracking, redneck from Alabama to be my best friend. Ladies and Gentlemen, may I present my partner and best friend…Dick Stuart."

Dick stood up to receive a warm round of applause. There was a noticeable murmur that started through the room.

"Isn't that Laura McNanty sitting next to him?"

The applause grew louder. The room was hoping Laura would stand to receive her applause. She never did. She merely waved at the audience and staunchly remained seated. She would do nothing to take anything away from Dick and Harry this night.

Harry then said, "Ladies and Gentlemen, you have made this a wonderful opening night for us here at Another Realm. I can only hope that you have had enough fun here tonight to continue to come back and see us again." I would like to say in closing, that I thank you, Dick thanks you, and Amber honey, goodnight." He closed the show the way he opened it. They went offstage after a rousing reprise of *That Long Lonesome Road*. Harry and the boys left the stage to a thunderous standing ovation and they were completely exhausted.

Dick was waiting backstage when he got there. "You did it, buddy," he said. "You brought the house down. I have never seen you better. C'mon, let's go get a drink."

"I'll be there in a little while, Dick," answered Harry. "I just need to clean up after the show. Get rid of this makeup and stuff," he said.

Harry had certainly not missed the fact that Laura was holding on to Dick's arm and it caused him to go into a spell of melancholy. He was happy for the possibilities it represented to Dick, but it made him miss Amber so much that it hurt. He went into the Amber room and sat in front of the waterfall. "It went great tonight, I thought," he said to the cascading water. "The band was great, too. What do you think?" Then he said, "You've gotta help me, Amber. This missing you is killing me and the only thing that will help me is the music." He then said in soft tone, "Please keep the music going. Without the music all I'll have left is missing you so much that I can't think of anything else. Keep the music going, baby because it's the only way I can make it without you."

He pulled himself together, blew a kiss at the waterfall and walked out into the party…

Chapter Seventeen

The party was going on in full swing when Harry got out to the front of the house. It was, "Great show, Harry" or "Hey, Harry, c'mere" or "Could I have your autograph, Mr. Foster?" It was an honest-to-God, full blown, opening night.

Harry went straight to Uncle Antonio's table. It was like a movie set from a Hollywood production of every gangster movie ever filmed. Big burly men wearing fancy suits. Some had shirts and ties and some with just polo shirts under their jackets. Harry believed that they carried other goodies under their jackets as well. That didn't upset Harry because he knew that as long as Uncle Antonio was in the room, everyone at his table would behave. Each one of these men had a gorgeous woman on his arm and the cigar smoke formed a blue ring around the entire table.

In the middle of the table flanked by two of the biggest men at the table sat Uncle Antonio. As Harry approached the table, Uncle Antonio stood up and bellowed, "Enrico, it is so good to see you!" Uncle Antonio came around the table and opened his arms to Harry. Harry obliged by walking into the circle that was his uncle's arms and accepted the kiss placed on his cheek. Harry knew that he owed a great deal to his uncle and was pleased to show him the proper respect.

"Uncle Antonio," said Harry, "I am so proud to have you here tonight. Anything you want tonight, Uncle Antonio, is on the house. Neither my uncle nor anyone who is with him tonight pays for anything," he instructed the waitress.

He sat down with Uncle Antonio and was introduced around the table. He met all the men and all the women. All were respectful, but cautious with him. They knew that Harry wasn't one of them, but that he was blood to the Don. That alone demanded respect from each and every one of them.

That is, all but one. His name was Franky Panzica and he didn't seem to feel that he had to show any particular respect for this "saloon singer." He thought he could treat him like every other show business "big ass" they had ever met.

"Hey, Foster," Franky said. "Great fuckin' show, but who the hell is that old fuck you got playin' drums? He's gotta be a hundred fuckin' years old!"

Harry started to field the question with charm because after all he was a friend of Uncle Antonio's, but he was interrupted. It was Uncle Antonio. "Hey, Franky," said Uncle Antonio, "C'mere." He nicely chided Franky by saying, "Don't talk like that to my nephew. It isn't nice."

Franky mumbled an apology, but Harry could see the smoldering eyes that blamed him for the embarrassment he had just endured.

Harry spent about a half hour with the table and excused himself to visit with other tables. That was fine with Uncle Antonio because his nephew had shown the proper respect by coming to his table first.

Harry had just turned his back and was starting to walk away when he heard a crash at the table. A bus boy had bumped into Franky Panzica and in anger, Franky had knocked the boy to the ground. Franky had picked the boy up by the front of his jacket and was about to slap him when Harry grabbed his arm.

"If you don't stop right now," hissed Harry, "I'll break this fuckin' arm of yours. He's just a kid for Christ's sake."

Franky was reaching inside his jacket when Uncle Antonio commanded, "Franky, cut it out! You've embarrassed us enough tonight with your bad manners!"

Franky removed his hand from his jacket and hissed at Harry, "You better hope you always have the favor of your uncle. If you should lose it," he said menacingly, "I promise I'll be the one to take you out." Nobody else but Harry heard the remark. Franky reached down and roughly took his date by the arm and said, "Let's get the fuck outta here!"

Harry walked over to the bus boy and straightened out his jacket and said, "Are you okay?"

"Yes, sir," stammered the bus boy. "I am real sorry, Mr. Foster," he explained, "but he turned around so fast, I couldn't get out of his way."

"That's alright, son," said Harry, trying to console the boy. "These things happen. Harry then added, "Just forget about it and keep your head up for the rest of the night."

Harry went over to Uncle Antonio to apologize.

Uncle Antonio just raised a hand and said, "Don't worry about it, Enrico. Franky is a good man to have around if there's trouble, but sometimes Franky IS the trouble. He then added, "My apologies to you, my nephew."

Harry excused himself once again and started to work the rest of the room. It was almost two o'clock in the morning when he got to Dick's table only to find that he had left about eleven-thirty with Laura. That both saddened and gladdened Harry. He was happy for his friend, but for himself…well.

It was three a.m. and everyone was just about finished cleaning up. The money had been counted, the glasses cleaned, floor swept, and everyone was saying goodnight to each other and complimenting each other on a job well done.

Harry was about to leave when a pretty blonde woman came up to him and said, "Mr. Foster, my name is Alisha Revson. I'm one of your bartenders, and I just wanted to thank you."

"For what?" asked Harry.

"That was my son you intervened for tonight," she said, "and there is no telling what might have happened to him if you hadn't helped."

"Oh, don't be silly," Harry responded. "That guy was just a jerk anyway."

"Nevertheless," she said, "I am grateful to you for your help."

"You're more than welcome...what did you say your name is?"

" Alisha Revson," she replied...

Chapter Eighteen

Alisha Revson had lived on the Keys for all of her thirty years. She was born Alisha Ryan to Meg and Tommy Ryan.

She was born at home and was the pride and joy of her father, but as a teenager, she was an absolute terror to her mother. She used to give her mother fits with back talk and boys. But when daddy came home…it was, "Hi, Daddy, glad you're home."

She would then go give her father a big hug and kiss. Tommy Ryan was absolute putty in his daughter's hands. It infuriated Meg, but Tommy just couldn't help himself.

Alisha had a normal childhood with all of the normal childhood diseases and cuts and bruises. She wasn't prepared for the bruise she received when she was seventeen, however. Her father had a sudden heart attack and was taken from her life. She loved her father totally and was devastated by the loss. At seventeen, she had just suffered her first major loss, and she reacted badly to it. She started drinking and she started drugging. It broke Meg's heart, but all she could do was endure it.

Alisha had become very pretty, and she was still so young. The boys certainly noticed how pretty she had become and there were always one or two of them hanging around. It drove Meg Ryan crazy. She tried to tell Alisha to be careful but it was like talking to a wall. Alisha was five foot five and had beautiful blonde hair. Her eyes were blue-gray and her smile was dazzling. Her figure stopped young men cold and it made old men remember. She was a knockout.

The traveling carnival had come to town that year. Working as a barker at one of the rides was Tommy Revson. The local girls all thought that he looked like James Dean. They all made jokes about what they would like to do to him and with him.

All her girlfriends made jokes, but Alisha was serious. She decided to set her sights on Tommy and she went after him with all of the ferocity of a seventeen year old in love. He never had a chance.

Tommy was twenty and from the moment he laid eyes on Alisha, he was in love. He didn't care that she was only seventeen. He didn't care that all the other guys working the carnival made fun of him for "robbing the cradle." The only thing that Tommy knew was that this girl was beautiful and he loved her.

When the carnival left town…so did Alisha. She and Tommy were married by one of the carnival employees. He was a Notary and had the legal right to do so. Meg Ryan tried to have the marriage annulled, but it was too late. When Alisha got pregnant, Meg gave up trying. Meg had visited them a number of times during the pregnancy and found Tommy to be, no matter how hard she fought against it, a very likeable guy and developed a warm affection for him.

Alisha and Tommy lived in one of the trailers that traveled with the carnival. Alisha had stopped drinking and stopped drugging from the moment she found out that she was pregnant. She didn't want anything to happen to her baby. She kept the trailer nice and clean and she and Tommy were very happy and obviously in love with each other. In spite of her young age, she blossomed as Mrs. Tommy Revson. Tommy, in spite of his young age, did everything he could to be a responsible husband and a soon-to-be father.

Alisha was very close to her due date when she got a call. It was the carnival manager. "Alisha, you've got to get down to the Midway," he said. "Tommy's been hurt in an accident and it's real bad. Hurry, as fast as you can," he added. The phone went dead. She rushed to the kitchen to turn the stove off, tore off the apron she was wearing, and ran outside to get down to the midway. Her trailer was about 150 yards away from the midway and she ran all the way.

When she got there she saw that the "Round-Up," a ride that was one of the favorites of the carnival goers, had collapsed. She saw that someone was trapped under some of the wreckage. She saw that that someone was Tommy.

Tommy was surrounded by twisted metal and a pool of gasoline that had come from the ruptured fuel tank that supplied the ride with power. There were at least five men trying to extricate Tommy from the wreckage. A spark from somewhere ignited the gasoline. The fireball was enormous and frightening. Tommy Revson and all five of his would-be rescuers died in a flash of orange flame.

A primal scream of horror rose from Alisha's throat. Its source was terror, fear, and disbelief.

"Nooooooooo!" screamed Alisha. "Tommy, please, no, no, no!! Oh, God, please, please, no!!" In that one moment, Alisha had become a seventeen-year-old widow and at the same time, clutched her stomach with the first wrenching labor pain that would make her a mother. Seven and a half hours later, Alisha gave birth to Tommy Revson Jr. Meg was by her side. When Alisha woke up, the first thing she did was ask for Tommy. The drugs they had given her for pain and stress still hadn't worn off. She was still disoriented.

"Tommy's gone," said Meg as gently as she could. "I am so sorry, Alisha," she added.

Reality forced its way past the drugs. She remembered the horrible truth and began to cry. Meg Ryan just held her little girl and let her cry and cry.

Mother and daughter raised Tommy together. What Alisha couldn't handle with the energy that was her youth, Meg could handle with the wisdom of years! The boy was growing up strong and healthy.

Fifteen years later, Alisha lost her mother to cancer. Except for Tommy Jr, Alisha was alone. She had lost everybody she ever loved tragically and prematurely and she vowed never to get involved again. It was just too painful when the losses came.

She had answered an ad for the opening of a new theme club called Another Realm. They were looking for help in all positions and she decided to go down and see if they could use some day help. She couldn't work at night because of Tommy Jr.

Dick was doing all the hiring. When he met Alisha and saw her beauty, he wanted her to work as a bartender. It was always good to have a good-

looking bartender. He had learned that basic lesson back at Fort Sill and the Holiday Inn days. He had a fleeting memory of Brenda.

A lisha told Dick that she couldn't take the job at night because of her son. Dick countered with, "Well, how old is he?"

"He's only fifteen," she said.

Dick then said, "He can bus tables at that age as long as you're on the premises. I promise we'll give him early shifts during the week and a place to crash if he gets tired." Dick didn't know what it was about this girl, but for some reason he just wanted her on board. After a little more selling, she agreed to take the job on a trial basis.

Alisha had never seen anything like this night. She saw celebrities everywhere. Some were famous and some were infamous. She saw people on this opening night of Another Realm that she had only seen on television, in the movies, or in magazines and newspapers. She was amazed.

It was about eleven o'clock at night. Harry Foster had just finished his show and had been talking to a group of dangerous-looking people in the front row right in front of the stage. She watched with a smile as her son Tommy worked his way around the table cleaning it off. The smile on her face froze as she watched her son bump into one of those dangerous-looking men. The man wheeled about and knocked her son to the floor. She started to run towards the table to help Tommy when she saw Harry Foster grab the man by the arm.

She got close enough to hear Harry Foster say, "If you don't stop right now, I'll break this fuckin' arm of yours."

She stood back and watched him brush the front of Tommy's jacket and tell him not to worry about it. She knew right then and there that was something special about Harry Foster Jr. It was three o'clock in the morning when she walked up to him and said, "Mr. Foster, my name is Alisha Revson. I'm one of your bartenders and I just wanted to thank you…"

Chapter Nineteen

As Harry walked into the club to start another evening, he was pleased to see that most of the staff was already hard at work. The maintenance people were scurrying about with mops and brooms. The wait staff was filling salt and pepper shakers and making sure the tables looked just so. The bartenders were filling juice containers, getting ice, and getting the bars ready for the night's business.

Harry noticed the boy he had helped last night. He was walking directly towards Harry. As the boy approached Harry, he started to speak.

"Mr. Foster, my name is Tommy Revson and I just wanted to thank you for last night. I was the kid who got in trouble with one of the patrons, when you…"

" I know who you are, son," said Harry. "I told you last night not to worry about it. That guy was a jerk anyway."

"Well, nevertheless," the boy went on, "I am grateful for your help."

Harry couldn't help but notice that the boy had the same speech pattern as his mother. *His mother? She doesn't look old enough to have a kid this age.* The thought bemused Harry. He wondered to himself why her age even occurred to him. He looked at the boy and thought, *He doesn't really look like his mother.*

Tommy Revson didn't look like his mother until you looked into his eyes. He had the same blue- gray eyes his mother had. When he spoke to you, those eyes held your attention just like his mom's. This also bemused Harry. He thought, *What the hell made me notice those eyes?* "You're doin' a good job, Tommy, said Harry. "Keep up the good work and don't worry about anything."

Almost as an afterthought Harry asked, "Hey, Tommy, how are your grades in school?"

"Oh, they're fine," answered Tommy, actually breaking out into a grin.

Harry was taken back. He certainly was his mother's son. The smile clinched it.

"Momma says I have a good chance at a scholarship if I keep up the good work." He then went on to say, "I better, because it's the only way we'll be able to afford to send me to college." Tommy blushed a bit. He thought that he might have said too much. He knew how his mother always refused to discuss family business with strangers.

"Never put your business in the street." Wasn't that how his mother put it?

Well, Mr. Foster wasn't exactly a stranger, thought Tommy. *He did save my life last night!* Tommy decided that he wouldn't tell his mother about this part of the conversation.

"Well, you take it easy, Tommy boy," said Harry.

Tommy broke into that grin again and Harry found himself thinking of the boy's mother again.

Harry was walking through the lounge still thinking of the boy's mother's smile when he all but knocked Alisha down. Harry was walking with his head down in thought and Alisha was backing out from behind the bar towing a utility cart. She was using the cart to re-stock the back bar and speed rack and was getting a fresh supply of ice. She had already cut up all the fruit and was just about ready for the night. Harry didn't see her coming and she didn't see Harry coming. The collision was inevitable.

When they bumped into each other it wasn't very hard, but it was at such an angle that Alisha began to lose her balance and was falling. Harry reached out without thinking, snaked an arm around her waist, and pulled her to him in order to stop her fall.

"Oh," she said and felt herself starting to lose her balance. As if by magic her momentum was stopped and she was being pulled upright and into some guy's arms. Her eyes widened when she realized the arms belonged to Harry Foster Jr.

"Oh, Mr. Foster," she cried. "I am so sorry! I should have been looking where I was going! Are you okay?"

"I'm fine," chuckled Harry. "How 'bout you? I guess we both should have been watching where we were going," he added. He still had his arm around her.

Realizing that he still had his arm around Alisha, he suddenly let go. She almost lost her balance again due to his sudden release and he had to grab her again.

"We probably ought to stop this," said Harry, chuckling. "Here's the deal: On the count of three, I'll let you go. Okay now, one, two three!" Harry let go and they both laughed.

Alisha flushed a bit and Harry was just the slightest bit uncomfortable, but managed to say, "There, we're both on our feet for now. Let's hope we can keep it upright for the whole night."

Harry, after checking that she was all right, excused himself and walked away to be about his business. He had a warm and not unpleasant sensation all about his body. It made him wonder just exactly what had gone on during the last few moments.

After assuring Harry that she was in fact okay, Alisha got back to the business of getting the bar ready for the night. She had a warm feeling, too and couldn't help but wonder what it would be like if Harry Foster really put his arms around her. She dismissed the thought and went about her business.

Chapter Twenty

Dick was up very early the next morning. He just couldn't sleep and what was more amazing, he felt that he had to get up. It was so amazing because in his bed slept Laura McNanty. Dick could not imagine how many a man had dreamed of waking up to find Laura McNanty in his bed. Dick sat on the deck with a cup of coffee in his hands. The deck was just off his bedroom and looked into a Florida sunrise that was spectacular. It was a sight that pleased him every time he saw it, but it held no charm for him this morning. On this particular morning he could look at the sunrise. He could then turn his head and look at the amazing woman who was sleeping in his bed. He found neither to be inspiring.

Dick and Laura had left the opening night of The Realm early because they couldn't keep their hands off each other. Dick knew he shouldn't leave early but he also knew that Harry would understand. This was Laura. This was Laura "friggin'" McNanty, for God's sake. This was Laura McNanty, the love of Dick Stuart's life.

They drove home to Dick's house. On the drive home they could not keep their hands off each other.

It was, "Oh, God, Dick, I've missed you." And, "Nobody can make me feel the way you do. Hurry, Dick. I'll die if I don't get you into a bed right now!"

They finally arrived at Dick's house. Dick went over to the bar and poured each of them a drink. The drinks were still sitting on the coffee table in the living room. Neither Dick nor Laura had even taken a sip out of them. They made love three times that night. Dick thought they had made love three times that night, but when his eyes clicked open at sunrise, he realized that they hadn't made love to each other at all, but in fact had just gotten laid three times. It left him saddened. He knew that he believed Laura McNanty to be the love of his life. In fact, he knew that Laura McNanty was the love of his life, but not the Ms. Laura McNanty of the silver screen.

"Hi, sailor," a voice said from behind him. He was looking at the sunrise and was startled by Laura's voice behind him. "Is it possible for a girl to get a cup of that coffee?" asked Laura.

He was pouring a cup of coffee for Laura when she came up behind him and encircled her arms around his waist. Dick could feel the heat of her body and the softness of her breasts against his back.

He turned and looked into Laura's eyes and started to say, "Laura, I don't know..." He was cut off by Laura.

"I know, Dick," said Laura, with a heartbreaking softness. "I know it's too late for us. I just hoped it wouldn't be," she added sadly.

"Laura," he started to say, but again was cut off by the soft voice of Laura McNanty.

"Dick, let me get this out," she said softly. "My entire career has been about you. If I needed a moment of passion for the screen, I thought about our night on the boat. If I needed joy, I would just remember breakfasts on the patio at Fortune Studios." She went on to say, "If I needed sadness or heartbreak, I would think about your face when I turned down your marriage proposal. But, if I needed to find silly laughter...I thought about the night you spent three hundred dollars trying to win me a teddy bear at the circus. She was laughing at the remembrance of that night and added, "but you finally won it!"

"I didn't though," Dick said.

"Whaddya mean," she countered.

"I sneaked the guy another hundred-dollar bill and he rigged it so I would win."

They both laughed at that.

"I figured that if I kept trying to win it fair and square, the cost could have been in the thousands," Dick finished.

Laura stepped back into Dick's arms. They held each other for a long time. They held each other as friends who had survived being lovers. They felt stirrings as they held each other but these feelings were different. They were feelings of warmth that only happen between friends. It was a feeling that made you feel as though your insides were swelling just a bit. It was a feeling that, if it could be photographed, would show that all your insides are smiling.It was with these feelings that they parted at the airport.

"Laura, if ever you need me for anything at all," Dick said lamely.

"If you don't let me go, sailor," Laura said in a wisecrack tone, "you're gonna have to take care of some needs that could get us both banned from this airport."

She knew that Dick would never see her all the way off. He had a superstition that wouldn't allow him to watch somebody leave because he believed it was bad luck. He would never watch anybody drive out of his driveway or get on a plane or for that matter even a ship. He had developed this habit from Harry Foster. He didn't necessarily believe it, but he always felt, "Why take a chance!" She held him in her arms for one long last moment. She turned him around and patted him on his butt.

"I love you, Dick Stuart," she said.

She watched with tremendous sadness as Dick walked away. She had come to find out if there was anything left between them and she got her answer.

The love affair between Laura McNanty and Dick Stuart was over.

When he finally turned to wave, she smiled, turned, and boarded the plane for Los Angeles, California, and back to Hollywood.

Chapter Twenty-One

As Dick drove back to the club, he was surprised at the feelings of peace he had within himself. He really hadn't realized how badly he needed to put the "Laura McNanty ghosts" aside. He was driving his car to work and for the first time in a long time, he felt good. He drove up to the front door of the club and handed his keys to the valet.

"Evenin', Mr. Stuart," said the valet.

"How ya doin'?" returned Dick.

Dick walked into the club just in time to see Harry with his arm around that pretty bartender he had hired.

What was her name? he thought to himself. "Alisha Revson," he said aloud to himself. It made Dick smile. He hadn't seen Harry anywhere near a woman in a long time. His heart sometimes broke for his friend. He hoped that it was a good sign. It was, after all, just a little shy of two years since the afternoon on the boat. Dick felt that Harry needed to move on, but he knew he couldn't force his friend in any way. Dick began to think that maybe he was right about his friend when he noticed Harry watching Alisha walk away. Harry had a way of watching a woman that told you what he was thinking. He hadn't seen that look on Harry's face for a long time.

"Howdy, partner," called Dick.

Harry turned and faced Dick. "Hey buddy, how you doin?" Harry returned.

"I see you've met Alisha," Dick said.

"I guess you might say that," returned Harry. "I wasn't looking where I was going and bumped into her. I almost knocked her down for Christ's sake."

Harry looked just slightly embarrassed and Dick laughed.

"What the hell are you laughin' at, you damn fool?" demanded Harry.

"Nothin' oh, nothin' at all," said Dick as he walked away.

The rest of the early evening went by quickly for the boys. Dick was tending to details in the office.

Harry, getting ready for the night's performance, was backstage going over a few things with Jocko on the piano. He wasn't up to snuff for this rehearsal because he kept losing his concentration. He found himself thinking about that cute bartender. He would be clipping along and suddenly he would be distracted by the thought of her. He seemed to get a warm feeling when he thought of her. He was confused. He cut the rehearsal short after Jocko said, "Earth to Harry Foster Jr. Come in, please."

Harry decided that he might like a drink before the show started. He never drank before going on stage, but decided he would tonight. There were at least six bars in the complex, but Harry decided on the one that Alisha was working at that was in the German motif for the night. It was also the farthest one from the Performance Center. He startled Alisha for the second time that night.

"Hi, Alisha," he said.

"Oh, Mr. Foster," she said, almost dropping the glass she was studiously polishing. "It's so nice to see you again. Can I do something for you?" she asked. "Can I do something for you!" she thought to herself. *Oh, for God's good graces, Alisha, why don't you just rip off your shirt!* she chided herself.

Harry smiled at her and said, "Well, the first thing you could do for me is lose the Mr. Foster stuff. I don't really like that." He added, "Although it does sound good when you say it. The second thing you could do is pour me a 'Buca on the rocks. I feel like having a cocktail before the show. How do you like working here, Alisha?" asked Harry.

"I love it Mr. Fost…er…Harry," she corrected herself. *This was going to take some getting used to,* she thought to herself. She loved the way her name sounded on his lips. "I get to meet all kinds of people and almost all of them are nice," she added.

"I thought you were assigned to the Performance Center," he said.

"No," she returned. "That was just for opening night."

"Did you like it there?" he asked.

"I did, very much," she said, "but they only need three bartenders and I was the fourth."

Then Harry said, "Maybe we could set up a rotation so that everybody could get to work the Performance Center at least once a week."

Harry turned that thought over in his mind and decided that it was a good idea. He would tell Dick…well…he would suggest it to Dick. He had learned a long time ago back at Fort Sill that you didn't tell Dick anything…you just suggested. Harry finished his drink. He really didn't want to leave, but he knew he had to. He really enjoyed being in this pretty girl's company and was just slightly uncomfortable. He didn't know why. He knew that there could be nothing to it.

I just like her, that's all, he thought to himself. As he turned away from her bar, he had the distinct feeling that she was watching him walk away. He was right.

Oh, Alisha, for crying out loud, she thought. *Why don't you just throw yourself at him? I'm sure that what Harry Foster Jr. wants is some bartender*

101

bimbo lusting after him! Settle down, Alisha, settle down, she thought to herself.

Harry searched for Dick and found him in his office. "Hey, Dickie boy," Harry started. "I was thinking...why don't we rotate the bartenders so they all get a chance to work the Performance Center. I was talking to one of the bartenders..."

"Oh really," said Dick, interrupting Harry. "Which bartender was that?"

"Why, what difference does that make?

"None, really," said Dick. "I was just curious. Was it Billy in the Italian room? Was it Moesha from the Jamaican room? It couldn't have been Alisha from the German room, could it?" he asked and started to laugh.

"Hey, why don't you go fuck yourself," said Harry. "I just thought it might be a good idea. If you don't like it...don't do it. I don't give a shit!"

"Okay, okay, Harry, I like the idea. Take it easy, buddy," Dick said and then started to laugh. "I was just askin'...that's all."

The music was vamping and the announcer had just brought Harry on stage. Harry was starting into his first number when he looked over at the bar. Alisha was there and Harry was happy. He was going to have to deal with these feelings somehow. He hadn't had them since he lost Amber. He would have to struggle with the guilty feelings he was having. He hadn't even thought about another woman since he lost Amber. He couldn't...he shouldn't...but this Alisha...

Chapter Twenty-Two

The night was over and the club had been packed again. Every room was filled to capacity and the show was a smashing success. People were coming in from all over the country to sample the fare and see the new Harry Foster Jr. show. The supper club called Another Realm was a smashing success.

Dick and Harry were lounging about the office. Dick was finishing up the paperwork for the night and Harry was just hanging out. They were both pretty pleased with themselves over their success. Each of them knew that they could not have done this alone, but needed each other. It was moments like this that caused them to marvel at the friendship that had started way back in 1965.

Harry then asked Dick, "Hey, listen, buddy, I don't know if I should ask you about this, but how did it go with Laura? I expected you to be talking about a wedding and you haven't said a thing. What's up?" he asked.

Dick said, "You know, buddy…sometimes things change. I thought that my life was over when I lost Laura. I thought that I could never love again and I certainly thought that I could never trust again." He went on. "I based my whole life on what it would have been like if Laura had said, 'Yes.' I thought that Laura was the only woman in the world I could love." He then stated simply, "I was wrong."

"We had a wonderful night and I can assure you that I love her still," Dick went on. "It became clear to me in the morning that although I loved Laura, I was no longer in love with Laura. We both realized that we could still be friends and, for that matter, lovers but that we were no longer in love with each other. At least not the kind of love that encompasses marriage. I decided that I still had a whole life to lead and I needed to be about that life."

Dick had no idea that his description of how he felt about Laura would impact Harry like a ton of bricks. It hit Harry so hard that it almost bowled him over. He was on his way to the Amber Room.

Harry sat in front of the waterfall for a long time. He was all alone. He just stared as the water cascaded down like the thousands of tears that Harry had shed over Amber. The water looked different tonight. It didn't remind him of tears but rather like diamonds. He looked at the water with different eyes. He looked at the waterfall as a thing of beauty tonight instead of a symbol of sadness.

Harry started to talk, "Hey, Amber, how you doin'?" he started. "Things have been goin' great here at the club. Ah, but you know that, don't ya? I imagine that you can see everything from up there, huh?"

"Amber," he went on, "I never had any idea what love was until I met you. I couldn't imagine that a woman like you could ever find a guy like me attractive, but you did. You took me when I was broken and fixed me. You patched me up, but instead of sending me on my way…you kept me. The feelings you brought out in me I didn't even think existed, or at least I didn't think that they could exist in me. I loved you so completely and so openly that every day was a holiday. Then a too tired trucker took you away from me and I thought my life was over. It has been for all practical purposes. I just go about my day doing the things that I have to and have very little joy in my life. You were my joy and you were taken away from me. You were taken away from me so suddenly that I thought I would die as well…just from the suddenness of it all. I found that there were so many things that I didn't know about you at the time because we hadn't been granted enough time for me to learn them. I didn't even know what faith to bury you in, for God's sake. I chose mine. I hope you don't mind. I promised you that I would love you forever and I intend to keep that promise. I will never ever forget your smile, your warmth, your love of life, and your caring for any unfortunate person who might have needed your help. I would marvel at how you could care for an injured animal with all of the same love and compassion that you took care of your patients. I never thought I could love anything like that until you showed me how."

"Amber," he went on. "There's this girl working here. Well, you've seen her. Her name is Alisha Revson. She kind of makes me feel the way you used to when we were together. I don't really know her yet, but I just have this feeling that she could make me happy. I'd like to get to know her, but I wouldn't want to do anything to hurt you or make you feel that I don't love you every bit as much as I always have.

"It was you that taught me that you could give all your love to somebody and still have it to give to others. I never could quite get the hang of that when you were trying to teach it to me, but now I think I understand. I love you every bit as much today as I did then and yet I feel that I could love this girl. If you can, Amber, honey, let me know how you feel about this."

Harry left the club and was walking towards his car. It was three a.m. He was tired and was ready to go home. A car was pulling out of its parking space. The car turned and headed towards Harry. Just as it approached Harry, the motor seemed to cough and then the engine died. The car rolled up to Harry and stopped dead right in front of him. It was an old 1967 Plymouth. Behind the wheel was Alisha Revson looking perplexed.

Harry looked to the heavens and said, "Amber, you gotta be kiddin' me!"

Chapter Twenty-Three

Harry walked over to the driver's side of the car and said, "Looks like you have a bit of a problem, eh, 'Lisha?"

Oh, my God, thought Alisha. *'Lisha.' Nobody has called me that since high school.* It sounded strange after so many years to hear her nickname, but it sounded wonderful, too. It sounded wonderful because Harry Foster Jr had used it. She had to remember to call him Harry from now on.

"Yeah, I guess so," admitted Alisha. "I just got this damned thing out of the shop too!" she added in an exasperated voice.

"Well, she is a bit long of tooth to still be on the road," said Harry.

He immediately wished he could take that back. He was afraid she might have taken it the wrong way and been insulted.

Instead she laughed and said, "Oh, boy, you're tellin' me."

Harry then said, "Listen, it's three o'clock in the morning and we'll never find a tow truck before dawn. He then added, "Why don't you let me drive you home?"

She agreed.

Harry got behind the old Plymouth and pushed the vehicle off into a parking space. He then went to his car, got paper and pencil and wrote a note for the police when they came to check on the vehicle. They were in the habit of checking vehicles that remained in the parking lot after closing. The note explained that someone would be by in the morning to take care of the car and get it moved. He signed it and was comfortable that it would be all right overnight.

He had gotten her seated in his car and had a strange, but not unpleasant feeling in his stomach. He hadn't had a woman this close to him since Amber and he wasn't quite sure how to handle himself. She gave him directions to her house and off they went.

They started talking immediately and felt as though they had known each other quite a long time. She immediately forgot that this was Harry Foster Jr. and that made him very happy. She immediately felt as though he was happy to be with her and that made her very happy.

Harry asked if she was in any hurry to get home. She said that she wasn't and Harry headed for the shore. They talked until the sun started to come up. It was now sunrise on Sunday morning on the Keys of Florida. When Dick and Harry opened the club, they had decided that no matter how much it cost, they would not open on Sunday. They wanted their employees to enjoy family and friends on at least one day a week. Both Dick and Harry remembered how much fun it was to be a kid and go on family outings on Sunday afternoons. They would not take that away from their employees.

"I was thinking about taking a ride to Miami this afternoon," said Harry to Alisha. "I was wondering if maybe you would like to come with me. That is, if you have time, of course," he added.

"Well, I was thinking about writing the Great American Novel this afternoon, but I could put that off until tomorrow," she said mischievously.

"So you'll go with me?" Harry asked.

"Yes, I'd like that," said Alisha.

He dropped her off at home and was headed back to his place for a little sleep. He stopped at a pay phone and called his mechanic.

"Joey," he said, "there's an old Plymouth in the parking lot at the Realm. If you fix it by tomorrow afternoon, there's an extra hundred in it for you. If you fix it before noon, there's another hundred for your wife, and if you fix it today, I'll throw in a hundred dollar savings bond for your son's college fund." He then added, "I don't care what's wrong with it or how much it costs. Make it ready for the races. I want it brand new."

"I'll make it so that Jackie Stewart couldn't find anything wrong with it, boss," said Joey. He than added, "And get the war bond ready because it will be finished before midnight tonight!"

Joey didn't really need the money. He had one of the most successful body and repair shops in all of Florida. He had worked hard and had become the repairman to the rich and famous. He did love Harry Foster though, and would do anything in his power to help him. It was Harry Foster who made all of the celebrities and the wealthy aware of "Joey the Mechanic" and they flocked to him with their cars. Joey's parking lot looked like a sales office for used Mercedes, Beamers, Ferraris, and any other absurdly priced automobile. Joey had become wealthy because of Harry Foster. Of course, that didn't mean that he wouldn't take the extra three hundred.

When Harry got home he stripped off his clothes and fell into bed. He was exhausted. He fell asleep immediately and started to dream about Amber. He always dreamed about Amber and it always awakened him with sadness. He would dream that they were about to go on a date. He would be driving over to her place to pick her up, but he would never quite get there. He would pull up in front of her house and see her in the back yard. He would try to get out of the car to go get her, but never quite could. He would awaken with the frustration of not having been able to reach her.

This dream was different. When he pulled up in front of her house, she turned and came over to him. She was as beautiful as ever.

She came over to Harry and took his face in her hands and said, "Harry, I'm happy here. This place where I'm at is a beautiful place, but it is only for those of us who have given up the place in which you live. You have a life to take care of and you should reach for as much of it as possible. I know how much you loved me and I know how much you love me still, and I need for you to understand how much I still love you." "I want you to be happy," she said. "This Alisha Revson is a special woman, Harry," Amber said. "She can make you happy and in turn that will make me happy. Remember, Harry," she added, "in this place you can give all your love to everybody and it feels wonderful." She then added, "You will love it too when you get here many, many years from now."

Amber still held Harry's face in both of her hands the way she did so many times when she and Harry were together and kissed him softly on the mouth. "Be happy, Harry," she said. "I want you to be happy because I love you still and I'll see you when you get here."

With that Amber just seemed to fade from the dream and Harry woke up. He had a tear in his eye, but a feeling of joy in his heart. He sat up in bed and said, "Thanks Amber…I do still love you…but thanks."

Alisha had slept for about two hours at the most. She would fall asleep and after what seemed to be hours, she would awaken to see that the clock on her nightstand had only moved ten or fifteen minutes. She was too excited to sleep. Tommy was laughing at his mother's manic behavior and said, "Ma, for God's sake, take it easy. He's just a guy."

"Whaddya mean?" she answered back. "Just a guy! Are you kidding me…that's Harry Foster Jr. I'm goin' out with on a real live date! Just a guy! Are you crazy?"

"Hey, Ma," said Tommy. "If you treat him like Harry Foster Jr., you won't see him again after today except at work."

Alisha looked at her son in amazement. "How did you get so smart in so little time?" she teased. She teased Tommy, but also knew he was absolutely right.

She settled down and went about the business of choosing her wardrobe for the day. She would choose and discard, choose and discard. "Too tight," she would say. "Too loose…makes me look fat…makes me look like a hooker."

She settled on green short skirt with a silken blouse of very light beige. She wore a gold chain that had a beautiful emerald hanging from it that Tommy's father had given her so many years ago. It was stunning against the light beige of the blouse.

Tommy looked at her and gave a low whistle, "Ma, you look great."

"Are you sure, Tommy?" she asked.

"I'm sure, Mom…you look fabulous," he said with finality.

She looked at her son and got just a bit misty. *He's so much like his father,* she thought. She walked over to him and gave him a kiss on his cheek and said, "Thanks, buddy, I needed that."

With that she heard a horn toot and when she looked out the window, she saw Harry jumping out of his car walking up the walkway.

What a day it was. They were all over Miami all day. Harry seemed to know somebody everywhere they went. He was welcomed with open arms at the Jockey Country Club and with the same open arms in the Barrios. They ate and they drank and they danced in the Barrio streets to street musicians who played the driving Latin beat. In the small jazz clubs, they danced to the sounds of jazz pianists. It was enchanting.

They had dinner aboard a night cruise ship. The meal that consisted of stone crabs, gazpacho, a Caesar salad, and a main course of beef and Maine lobster tail was absolutely fit for royalty. The wines were the best the ship had to offer.

They took their coffee on deck. They had both ordered espresso coffee and Sambuca. The coffee was hot and robust and the snifters were filled with the licorice liqueur of Italy and, of course, the traditional three coffee beans.

By an arrangement with the crew, they had this little corner of the deck to themselves. They settled back in chaise lounges to enjoy a four-hour cruise straight into the famous Florida full moon.

He reached over to find her hand. She gave it willingly. He said, "Look, Alisha, I'm not very good at this anymore. It's been such a long time since I've been out on a date, I'm not really quite sure how to act."

She smiled and said, "You're doing fine, Harry. I have never had such a wonderful day."

She put her hand on the back of his head and kissed him lightly. She moved back and looked into his eyes and kissed him again. This time the kiss was more intense. Harry responded. They touched each other tentatively at first and then with great hunger. Each thrilled to the other's responses and was surprised at their own.

"Are you sure about this 'Lisha'?" breathed Harry.

"I've never been so sure of anything in my life," she answered back breathlessly. "What about you?" she asked.

He answered by kissing her more deeply than she had ever been kissed in her life. On the deck of that cruise ship, as if they were the only people on board, Harry and Alisha made love to each other. They made love to each other and washed away all of the pain and sorrow of past losses and in homage to all of the possibilities of a future life. They made love to each other because they were in love with each other and they both knew it.

It was Sunday night and Dick had been in the office for hours. He hadn't accomplished anything. He had been staring at the phone for three hours trying to work his courage up. He had been thinking about this since the day he let Laura McNanty get on that plane for Hollywood. He knew what he needed to do if he ever expected to be happy.

He picked up the phone and dialed...405-555-3241. A soft mid-western voice answered.

"Hello."

A flood from the past came rushing back. Nights at the Holiday Inn, Fort Sill, singing in the Lion's Den with Harry and Dale. "Brenda? It's me...Dick."

Chapter Twenty-Four

The pause on the other end of the line was agonizing to Dick. After what seemed to him to be at least eternity, Brenda finally replied with, "Hello, Dick."

Dick asked awkwardly, "How have you been?"

"How long has it been, Dick? Seventeen years or so?" she quizzed in a very noncommittal tone.

Sensing that the conversation was not going well, Dick decided to come directly to the point. "Look, I've got some business in Oklahoma City in a day or two. I thought that perhaps I could get down there for dinner one evening and we could bring each other up to date."

There was another pause and Brenda responded nonchalantly, "Sure, why not." She then added, "Call me when you get to Oklahoma City."

"Okay, I will. Bye." Dick put the receiver down and thought how stupid he felt and how amateurish he must have sounded.

Dick had just accepted a cocktail from the stewardess when he thought again of the phone conversation with Brenda two days prior. He hadn't the courage to tell her that he was coming strictly to see her. It was safer, he thought, to lie about a business trip to deflect his burning desire for a reunion. It was a good thing, too, since she didn't exactly overwhelm him with her warmth.

"Well, what did you expect, dumb ass?" he wrestled with himself. "You walked out on her!" He just felt like a big jerk.

His thoughts drifted back to twenty years earlier when he would catch "med evac" to come and go on military leaves. He never paid a dime to travel. That was one good thing his old man had taught him. *About the only good thing, come to think of it,* he thought to himself. Now he flew strictly first class. "What a difference money and success can make in one's life," he concluded to himself. On the other hand, he wasn't that happy so what difference did it make? He thought of his friend Harry and how he had turned his life around and he was so very happy for him.

After the plane was down in Oklahoma City, Dick called Brenda from the airport to set up their rendezvous in Lawton. They decided to meet at Wright's Steak House. It was one of Dick and Harry's favorite spots when they were stationed there.

At seven that evening, he rolled the rental car into Wright's and went immediately to the cocktail lounge and ordered a Cuba Libre. The place had been expanded and refurbished since he'd seen it last, but one thing had not changed: the telltale and delightful aroma of U.S. prime beef emanating from the kitchen grill.

Dick was sitting in a position in the lounge from which he had a full view of the traffic coming in the front door. He was not surprised to see her coming into the softly lit club. What did surprise him was the way she looked. She wore her hair up and in doing so, gave her perfectly oval face all the attention. Her jewelry was modest and in good taste. She wore a smart business suit that covered a soft, off white, blouse. There was nothing to hide her full and beautifully shaped figure—although Dick felt a twinge of disappointment because so much of her was covered. This negative thought vanished when she appeared next to him and the diffused light cascaded down one side of her unblemished face. He was awestruck and it showed.

"Hi, Dick," she said in a polite and business-like voice.

"Age has been so kind to you, Brenda," he stammered. "You're even more beautiful than I imagined."

"Thank you. I see that you haven't lost any of your charm, Dick," Brenda replied.

"Please sit down," Dick said. "What can I get for you?"

"A glass of white wine will be fine," she answered.

Dick thought that the ice was beginning to break as he ordered her a glass of Chablis. Well, at least he hoped he sensed a thaw in her icy behavior.

After a drink and some small talk, Dick asked, "Please tell me about your life after…"

She interrupted, "No, you go first."

"Well, alright," and he related the whole story in great detail. Starting the story in Chicago and ending it in south Florida. They moved to the dining room after Dick finished his story and ordered their food.

Following a wonderful steak dinner topped off with a Crème de Menthe Frappe, Dick said, "Now it's your turn, Brenda."

"I'm afraid my life has not been nearly as exciting as yours, Dick," she began. "After you lef—"There was a pause and Dick could see there was still pain in her heart. She composed herself and continued. She told of a marriage that followed two months after he and Harry had left for the road.

He was a G.I. by the name of McLeod. He was soon shipped to Vietnam, as most were in those days. A son was born while he was away and life was a struggle for her from that point on. When he came home, the war had changed him in the worst possible way. She took his alcoholism and abuse for as long as she could.

When she could take no more she took her son and moved into a battered women's shelter. She had hit rock bottom. She was determined to bring herself back if for no other reason than for her son.

She got her job back at the Holiday Inn and took college courses at night to further her education. It was rough, but not nearly as rough as her days in the Godforsaken shelter.

Finally, and due to her almost manic perseverance, she got her real estate license and the rest was history.

She had made herself over into a highly successful businesswoman and was respected in the community. She had also raised a wonderful son on her own and he was now her best friend.

Dick had listened intently in silent admiration as this magnificent example of a woman finished her story. He was so ashamed of himself as he choked, "Brenda, can you ever forgive me?"

She looked down at her drink for a moment and then said, "Oh, Dick, that was a million miles ago and a lot of water under a great big bridge."

He knew that she was not being truthful.

It was clear to Dick that it was time to conclude the evening so he asked, "May I follow you home to make sure that you get there safely?"

She replied in the negative and appeared uneasy over the offer.

"May I call you again, Brenda?" he asked.

"I think we should just end this here, Dick" she replied.

It took him by surprise and before he could speak she added, "It was good seeing you again." She wheeled and left the restaurant. Dick hastily looked at the tab and wadded some bills. He threw them down on the table. He knew he had left enough to more than cover it. He hurried out the large swinging doors to see Brenda speeding west down Cache Road. He couldn't get over what had just happened and he sensed that something just wasn't right.

The next morning as he was checking out of his hotel, he was determined to make one more attempt to make things right with

Brenda. If nothing else, he wanted to tell her how he felt about her before she had a chance to throw up a detour. It was easy enough to locate her home and he was soon motoring in that direction.

He cruised the subdivision until he found the residence at the end of a cul-de-Sac. It was a spacious and well-landscaped ranch style home and her car as well as another was in the driveway.

"Uh oh, looks like she might have company." As he proceeded up the sidewalk toward the front door, it suddenly opened.

Dick was stunned when he saw the full frontal view of a teenaged boy before him. In a hoarse voice he asked, "Are you Ms. McLeod's son?"

The young man replied, "Yes, sir. I'm Rick McLeod. Are you looking for my mom?"

Dick could not answer. He was looking directly into his own eyes—years ago when he was a soldier at Fort Sill, Oklahoma!

Chapter Twenty-Five

"Hey, are you all right, mister?" asked the boy.

Dick was staring at the boy as if he had seen a ghost.

"Mister, hey, mister," the boy repeated.

The roaring in Dick's ears was like a freight train. He felt as though he might fall down. He knew in an instant what the great truth of his life was. He had walked away from his son. The fact that he didn't know it was no comfort. All these years Brenda had kept this secret.

"Did anybody know that this boy with the name of Rick, or Richard Mcleod, should have been named Rick Stuart? Did the G.I. Mcleod have any idea that this boy was not his son?" He had so many questions. Seventeen years of absence from this boy's life made even the simplest things of an ordinary life of prime importance to Dick. Did he have his tonsils removed? Has he got a steady girlfriend? How are his grades in school? How tall is he? What's his favorite color, favorite ice cream, and favorite baseball team? So many questions!

Oh, my God, Dick thought to himself. *What am I gonna do?*

He looked at this skinny six-foot boy with wonderment. He had light brown hair and eyes that seemed as though they could look right through you. The light brown hair fell across the boy's forehead and looked as soft as silk. The boy had a smile on his face, but it was used to cover concern for this stranger who was standing in his driveway.

"Hey, mister, are you okay?"

"I'm fine," said Dick, finally pulling himself together. "Is your mother home?"

"Yeah," said the boy, "she's in the house. You want me to go get her?"

"No, that's okay, son. I'll go get her myself," said Dick. *Son,* thought Dick to himself. *My God, can it be true?*

He turned to walk up to the house when he saw Brenda standing in the doorway. Her look was one of defiance, but it had traces of fear in it as well. He could see that this wasn't going to be easy for either of them and he knew he had to be careful how he handled the situation. He knew that the boy in the driveway was his son, but if Brenda didn't want to admit it, there was nothing he could do about it. He had, after all, been Rick Mcleod for his entire life and it would be tricky business to try to walk into this boy's life after seventeen years. He didn't know what to feel or what he was going to say as he walked up to the doorway where Brenda was standing. He had feelings of guilt and anger and pride and, above all else, confusion. He didn't know what he was supposed to be feeling right now.

"What am I supposed to do now, Brenda?" he asked.

"About what?" she returned.

"Oh, c'mon, Brenda, you know very well what I'm talking about. Why didn't you tell me?"

"Tell you what?" she insisted.

Dick was beginning to lose patience. "Why didn't you tell me we had a son?" He said this in a more demanding tone.

Brenda was just as adamant. "I don't know what you're talking about," she answered back.

"Now I understand what last night was all about—the way you took off like a scared rabbit when I suggested we get together again. Did you really think that once I got here that I wouldn't find out?"

There was ice in her voice when she said, "Find out what, Dick?"

Dick was taken back by the coldness in her voice, but persisted by saying, "Are you gonna try to tell me that the boy who just left the driveway is not our son?"

"Yes, that's exactly what I'm gonna tell you," she said frostily. "I left that boy's father because he was a drunk and he was an abuser. I've been raising that boy on my own ever since. We've done just fine without him around here and for that matter we've done just fine without the 'Great Dick Stuart' around here as well! Do you really think that I heard about your life story for the first time last night when you told me about it?

"I've followed your life along over the years and know what you've been doing. I know about your law degree and I know about the business in Florida with Harry and I know about the failed relationship with Laura McNanty. I followed you throughout the newspapers and all the articles written about you and Harry and fantasizing that it would be wonderful if I were with you. When you're in a shelter for battered women, what you do mostly is daydream. Ricky would be on the floor with a toy that someone had given him or just throwing a baseball up in the air playing catch by himself and I would be on the bed poring over all the papers just looking for anything about you and Harry. It was one of those mornings that I decided that I was not gonna let this get me down. I was going to go to school and make something of myself! Like Scarlett O'Hara, I promised myself that I would never be hungry again! I got my realtor's license, opened my own business, and now I own the top realty company in the Lawton area. I did it alone—just Rick and me and I did very well indeed, thank you very much!"

Although she was crying now, she was absolutely defiant when she said, "He's not your son, Dick! He's my son!"

"What the hell is this 'I am woman, hear me roar' bullshit. Look, I don't blame you for being pissed off at me, but for Christ's sake, I didn't know. If you had let me know about it I would never have left with Harry. When I called you up last week, I lied to you."

She interrupted him with a sarcastic, "Oh, that's a first."

"Cut it out, Brenda," he said with an exasperated tone. "I lied when I said I had business here. I don't have any business here. I just wanted to see you. No matter what I've done or where I've been or with whom I've been, I have never stopped loving you. I came to Oklahoma because I couldn't stay away from you any longer. I just needed to see you. I have never stopped loving you for even a moment."

"Oh, really?" she said. "You're so crazy about me that you could only take the separation for seventeen years?"

"Brenda, please," Dick said softly.

Dick looked into the eyes of this woman he loved so very much and thought to himself that he saw something in her eyes other than the defiance she had been showing him throughout this entire conversation.

He decided to take a chance at this point. "Brenda, please let me try to make up for the time we've lost. You and me and our son."

"He's not your son!" she fired back. "He's my son!"

"Brenda," Dick said, "you never told me what you husband's first name was. What was it anyway?"

"John," she answered back. "Why?"

"Then why did you name the boy Richard?"

Brenda sat on the steps and began to cry.

Chapter Twenty-Six

Dick moved close to her and reached for her hand while she continued to cry, "Let's go inside," he whispered. With that, he helped her up, steadied her, and accompanied her through the front door of the home. He gently escorted her to the handsome leather sofa and eased into it. He put his arm around her and said, "It's okay to cry…let it out, sweetheart."

She laid her head on his shoulder and kept crying until she could cry no more. It was obvious to Dick that she was dressed and ready to go to work and Rick was probably leaving for school when he drove up, but she was indeed a mess now. The mascara flowed out of her eyes and streaked black down her cheeks. He felt so sorry for her. There was silence for several more minutes.

In a broken and fragile voice Brenda said, "I…I didn't want you to stay just because I was pregnant. I wanted you to stay because you wanted me." The crying began again.

Dick felt a strange peace in what was just said because he knew that simple statement validated his fatherhood. With a love that he had never felt in his entire life and tears streaming down his face, he took her chin in the cup of his trembling hand, turned her beautiful countenance to his, and softly kissed her lips. He looked into her eyes, which had changed to a stunning shade of green from all the crying and gently said, "I have come to realize as I have matured over the years, that the life I left to find so long ago was right here with you. My darling, I love you more than anything or anyone on this earth." He kissed her.

She kissed him back with a tenderness that could only come from someone deeply in love…and so, in unspoken unison, they took it to the highest and most sacred level…they shared each other's body with a passion that was totally unfamiliar to both.

When it was over, they just held each other for a while, not wanting their oneness and the solitude to end. Finally, it was Dick who spoke. "Brenda, what are we going to do?"

After a minute, she replied, "I think we should just back off from each other for a while…to assess things in a clearer light."

Dick could not believe what he was hearing. They had come this far together and now there would be a time out? "Honey, I don't want back off…I want to a part of your life and Rick's as well."

"Let's discuss this later, Dick," Brenda suggested. "I should have been in my office an hour ago. I have some appointments I must keep."

Sensing that it was time to "fold 'em," as they say, he agreed. "How about dinner tonight?" he asked.

"Tell you what…let's make it breakfast tomorrow morning, okay?" she replied.

Trying to hide his disappointment, he agreed, feeling that was better than nothing.

"Meet me at the IHOP on Cache and 54th at eight o'clock."

"I'll be there," he said, and after a brief hug, left Brenda's house.

As he was driving back to his hotel, he thought to himself, *Richard, my boy, you have got a hold of one independent woman.* And man, how much he admired her for that quality.

He would not sleep well that night.

He was on pins and needles when he entered the revolving door of the restaurant the next morning. He was a little early, so he was seated in as private a booth as possible and ordered black coffee.

He didn't have to wait too long before she slid in the opposite side of the booth and looked at him without a trace of what happened between them twenty-four hours earlier. She was dressed to the nines and was just as striking as yesterday and the day before.

"I think I owe you the truth," she said, "about Ricky."

Dick sat up alertly and responded with a sincere, "Thank you."

"John McCleod was overseas when Ricky was born and he never knew Ricky wasn't his. I never really loved him, but thought that I could learn to, after a time. It might have happened had it not been for John's Vietnam experience."

She went on to say," I divorced him when Ricky was five, and haven't seen him since."

"He never paid one shred of support and God knows I needed it but, you know, now I am so grateful that he didn't."

"Brenda...I am so proud of what you've done," Dick began. "You have done so well, that I'm not so sure I would have made a difference in, may I say, our son's life. I can fully understand you wanting to protect him from this trauma, but understand this— I love you with all my heart. I came out here to see you, not knowing we had this beautiful child in our lives. I consider him a wonderful surprise. In some way, I want to make a difference in his life, whether he knows it or not. But just as importantly, I want you in my life. I would give up everything for you, my love."

She looked at him with those haunting eyes and said quietly and measured, "Dick...take me to your hotel room...now."

Without so much a word, they were out the door, in Dick's car, and headed to the hotel.

There were no words as the two lovers hurtled down 54th and turned on to 7th Avenue. Dick wheeled into valet parking at the hotel. They had entered the lobby and were headed toward the elevator when they were intercepted by the bell captain.

"Mr. Stuart? Telegram for you, sir." Dick tipped him and opened the envelope. It read: "Dick (stop) there has been a fire (stop) need you here ASAP (stop) Harry"

Chapter Twenty-Seven

Harry just sat in the car and stared at the hulk that was once the site of the Another Realm Entertainment Complex. He was stunned and couldn't believe what he was looking at. The one time magnificent building had been reduced to a still smoldering shell. Everything inside the building had been destroyed. The small little "chapel" that he had dedicated to Amber was now nothing more than another smoldering section of the complete destruction wrought by the fire. He was completely broken-hearted to look at such an unbelievably sad sight.

He was also furious. The destruction was complete and it was no accident. Someone or some group of people had set this fire. It was too complete in its savagery. He knew that someone was responsible for this, but he just couldn't imagine why. He would find out.

I'll damn sure find out! he thought to himself.

It had started in the Jamaica Room. It was there that the destruction was most complete. It didn't start slowly. It started with an explosion. The person or persons who started the fire had poured gasoline everywhere and with no attempt to hide the fact that it was arson, had set a timer to go off at three a.m.

The beautiful tropical birds that lived in the room lay dead in the ashes and so too, Moesha, the beautiful black woman who was the manager of the Jamaican Room. She was so proud of being the manager that she never left until everything was in perfect order. She always arrived early for work and always stayed late to make sure that the Jamaican Room was always perfect for the night's guests.

"Just because of you, Moesha, I will find out who did this," Harry said aloud.

The "Firestarter" sat on his balcony and giggled to himself. From his condominium he had a perfect view of Another Realm. He was there on his balcony at three a.m. when the first explosion occurred. It gave him a feeling that could only be described as ecstasy. The feelings were more intense than he had ever realized with any of the hookers that were his love life. He had no concept of what a real human relationship was. He was envious of anybody who had one.

He hated Harry Foster because of his relationship with the Alisha from the Circus Room. He had hated Amber Adkinson, Harry Foster's fiancée, because of how happy those two were together. He thought that when he had rigged Amber's car to slowly lose brake fluid and go out of control on the highway, the insufferable Harry Foster would be brought down a peg or two. The fact that she actually died in the crash was like a gift from heaven. He had to have three separate hookers that night to satisfy the lust her death created in him. He was furious that it only took such a short time for the "wonderful" Harry Foster to find somebody else to love.

He was pushed to action when he saw how happy they were together. He would make them pay. He most certainly would.

Alisha was supposed to be in the Circus Room when the fire broke out, but she had left earlier in the evening to go out somewhere with Harry. It was a disappointment to the "Firestarter," but at least that black bitch was dead. He hated her, too, for no other reason than she was black.

He hated her for the same reason he hated Catholics, kikes, spics, and that group he saved most of his hatred for—the "faggots." He hated them all just because they were there. He sometimes wondered to himself why he hated the faggots most of all, but he would just shrug it off.

The investigators would find Moesha gagged and bound to a bar stool. She, too, was soaked in gasoline.

The Realm burst into flames. He thrilled to each additional explosion. He knew that the arson would be discovered immediately by the investigators, but they would have absolutely no reason to come looking for him. It wasn't until five a.m., when the last room that had burst into flames—the Amber Room— was being brought under control by the fire department that he decided to go out to "Little Havana" and find some of his favorite "playthings."

He had found three of them that night. He had sex with three hookers from the hours of 5:30 a.m. to 6:30 a.m. Only the fire of sex could douse the lust the burning of Another Realm had created in him.

He had each one of them outside. He had taken them from behind as they leaned against one of the picnic tables in the park. He took them roughly and without compassion. He smoked a great Cuban cigar all the while.

The last one felt his passion the most. At the very moment of climax, he put his lit cigar out on the poor girl's rump. She tried to protest, but he held her fast to him with one arm and didn't stop until both his passion and the cigar were completely doused. He gave this girl a thousand dollars and left her crying on all fours in the park. He just dropped ten one hundred dollar bills in front of her and walked away without ever looking back. He was lighting up another long Cuban cigar.

Harry was lost in thought when he saw somebody approaching from across the street. It wasn't until the figure got all the way up to the car that Harry recognized him.

"This is just horrible," said the man. "I am so sorry, Mr. Foster."

Harry was relieved to see someone that he knew and simply said, "Thank you very much."

"It isn't much, Mr. Foster, but these are genuine Cuban cigars. Can I offer you one?"

Harry looked at the man and said, "That's very nice of you. Yes, I would like one…thanks."

Chapter Twenty-Eight

Dick's mind was racing as he disembarked at Miami International. It had been years since he had to deal with problems of this magnitude. He fully realized that it was his duty to be at his best friend's side at this time of upheaval, but his heart was still in Oklahoma.

Things were just left up in the air with Brenda, although she fully understood his need to leave immediately. Still, he felt the disaster at Key Largo threw a damper on the progress toward a possible reconciliation with her—and then there was the matter of his new-found son. He forced all of this out of his mind for the time being. He recognized that his full attention was needed at the company.

This situation upset Dick greatly, but he knew this would have a devastating effect on Harry because since the death of Amber, the Realm was his whole life. It was the club that pulled Harry from the abyss of despair and, in all likelihood, saved his life.

Benny Rhodes, one of the club's best employees, met Dick at the gate and escorted him to the company van for the one-hour drive to the Keys.

"How bad is it, Benny?" Dick asked, almost reluctantly.

"Pretty awful, boss. It just about wiped everything out. The only reason it didn't get the van was 'cause I had taken it home to get it serviced this morning," he related. "We lost the limo, though," he added.

"Does anyone know what caused it yet, Benny?"

"No, sir. I haven't heard."

Dick glanced at his watch and made note that it was four p.m. "Better take me directly to Mr. Foster's home," he directed.

Dick saw Harry's Jag in the large circular driveway in front of his residence.

"You can leave for now, Benny, but hang loose. We might need you and the van."

"Okay, boss. See you later." He drove away, leaving Dick facing the dreaded walk to the massive front door made from the deck of a 1921 schooner, once a part of the Hearst Empire. Dick smiled slightly, as the door reminded him that his buddy always went first class, or not at all.

He rang the door bell as was his custom. It was out of respect for the man that he would never just walk into Harry's house.

Directly, it was Alisha who opened the door slightly and peeked out into the bright sunlight. She was squinting, but Dick could quickly see in her eyes the sadness that had overcome her.

"Oh, my God, Dick…I…" she broke down like he had never seen her before. He held her for a moment until she was somewhat composed. "He needs you, Dick…he really needs you. Come…please."

Alisha took him by his hand and led him to the very back of Harry's home to the kitchen. He wasn't prepared for what he saw next.

To say that Harry looked a mess was a gross understatement. It took Dick back to the years before Harry's rehab.

On the kitchen table was a bottle of Tangueray, which was almost empty, and a single shot glass. In all his years with his friend, Dick had never seen him drink gin. He looked as if he hadn't slept in a day or two, which was actually the case, as he learned later. Harry's head lay on the table with his face away from

Dick and Alisha. The rest of the table was entirely covered with the blueprints of their club in a state of disarray.

"He's been this way for the past couple of hours," Alisha advised. "He won't listen to me or go to bed."

Her voice trailed off as Harry began to come to. When he turned his head in their direction, Dick was looking into the eyes of a beaten man.

When he realized Dick was there, Harry staggered to his feet and cried, "Oh, Jesus, Dicky…they got us, those sons-a bitches…they got us!" He started crying uncontrollably, almost to the point of convulsions. The tears were a mixture of sorrow and blinding fury.

The alcohol is really working on him, Dick thought as Harry stumbled into Dick's arms.

"Come on, pal…come with me," Dick said as he helped him into the den to oversized sofa. Harry collapsed on the couch and Dick placed his legs on it as well so that he now lay prone. Alisha brought two pillows and a blanket and together they put Harry to bed on the sofa. Alisha began straightening and tidying up.

"Alisha, is your son okay?" asked Dick.

She replied, "Yes…he's staying with friends."

"Well, listen…I'm going to take Harry's car and run home for a while. Will you be okay here?"

"Yes, Dick…no way would I leave him now," she answered.

Dick was heading for the door and said, "Call me at the condo if you need me." With that, he left.

Dick wheeled the big Jaguar out of the driveway and headed for the Realm.

When he came upon it, it was as if napalm had hit it. It was worse than he had imagined and he still didn't know of the death of an employee. The whole scene was enclosed in police tape and he figured the authorities were on top of it. There was no reason for him to linger there. He had a lot of work to do.

Dick was sharp. He was the quintessential businessman. Every single creditor, supplier, agent, and business record was backed up on microfiche and categorized at his condo. He would spend the remainder of the evening preparing a business plan from the next day forward, including the filing of what would be an extensive insurance claim.

He attacked the work with a zeal he had not felt in a long, long time. It was midnight when it dawned on him he had a lover who had probably been waiting for his call.

"Honey, I'm sorry to be so late calling you, but I'm up to my neck in alligators," he said into the phone.

"Dick, I'm so glad you called. I was beginning to worry," Brenda replied.

Dick briefly filled her in, including the ordeal with Harry. "I hope to God that I can pull him out of this," he lamented. "Lucky for him he's got a good woman behind him," he added. There was a brief pause and Dick said, "And I'm thankful that you are back in my life, darling." Another pause and, "I love you, Brenda."

An even longer pause, then, "And I love you too, Dick. Goodnight."

That was all Dick Stuart needed to motivate him even further. When he laid the receiver down, he walked over to his bar and poured a shot of Finlandia. He looked in the mirror behind the bar and stared at himself. He lifted his glass in a self-salute, swallowed the vodka, and said with resolve: "If the Phoenix arose from the fuckin' ashes, then so can we…

Chapter Twenty-Nine

Harry's gin-induced sleep was tormented. He had recurring dreams of the fire and Moesha. He dreamed that he was reaching for Moesha when the fire came and drew her back. Moesha. That beautiful brown girl that was so thrilled to be the manager of the Jamaica Room. The girl who worked so hard to prove herself worthy of the job, died because of that dedication. Harry used to tease her by saying, "Someday this workin' so late is gonna kill ya, Moesh'."

She would laugh and say, "Mr. Foster, a little hard work never killed anybody!" They would both laugh, and now she was dead because she worked late.

Alisha was watching him toss and turn about the couch where she and Dick had laid him and her heart was breaking. Suddenly, Harry went completely still and a calm came across his tortured and tormented face. The stress lines in his face relaxed and it seemed to Alisha that there was a slight smile on playing on Harry's lips. Then his brow knitted and it was as though he was listening with great intensity to someone. She watched in amazement and was grateful that the torturous dreams Harry was suffering had apparently ended…

Suddenly, in Harry's dreams of the fire and Moesha's death, came Amber. She walked out of the fire and straight at Harry. Harry remembered that look from his "Therapy Days." He was suddenly relaxed. He knew that Amber would straighten this out for him.

"What the hell are you doing?" demanded Amber. "You have a bit of a problem and you're gonna fall apart again? I won't stand for it, Harry! I told you the last time that we talked that you had a life to lead and that you should reach for all of it that you can. "I told you that Alisha is a very special woman and that she can make you happy. I didn't tell you that it was okay to make her a nursemaid to a beaten drunk. You've got Dick Stuart in your life. He would lie down and die for you. He has found himself again with Brenda, but he had to come back and play wet nurse to you because you were upset. He had to come back after finding out about his son because his buddy Harry was depressed!"

Harry looked at Amber with wide eyes and she said, "Yeah, that's right, he's got a son. He can't be with that son though 'cause he's gotta be here with you. He had to walk away from Brenda again because Harry needed him! For Christ's sake, Harry…grow up, will you!"

Alisha watched in amazement as Harry's face suddenly broke into a complete smile.

Harry thought to himself as he continued to dream. *She is the only person in the world who can talk to me that way.*

"Now listen, mister," Amber continued. "I can't keep coming back here like this to bail you out of your Major Manic Moments forever. I'm not supposed to do this. I'm supposed to let you figure all this out by yourself. I'll do this one more thing and then you have to figure it out for yourself." With that she reached into the fire and pulled by the hand, Moesha! There she stood in all her brown beauty with a dazzling smile on her face and said,

"I'm happy here, Mr. Foster. Don't worry about me. We'll see ya in a bunch of years from now."

With that the dream faded and Alisha watched Harry's face become as calm and placid as a lake in the morning. She didn't know what happened, but she was grateful for it anyway.

When Harry awoke, he was alone on the couch. He knew he should be hung over very badly, but he felt refreshed and alive. He smiled again when he thought of the scolding Amber had given him last night. Suddenly his thoughts stopped him dead in his tracks. "A son?" He remembered what Amber had told him in his dream and wondered if it could possibly be.

He went to the phone and dialed 405-555-3241.

"Hello," said a sleepy voice.

"Brenda? This is Harry Foster. Please forgive me for calling you at this time of day. I know it is terribly early."

"Has something happened to Dick?" she interrupted. She was suddenly frightened that she might lose Dick again. She didn't think she could take that again.

"No, no," said Harry. "He's fine. I was told last night that you and Dick had had a son…is that true?"

"He told you already?" Brenda asked.

"No, he didn't tell me…Amber did."

"Amber?" asked Brenda. "Isn't that the woman I read about in the papers who you were supposed to marry?"

"Yes, yes," he interrupted. "Never mind about that. Is it true?" he insisted.

"Yes, it is," she said quietly.

"Holy Smoke," said Harry. "That's wonderful! Dick told me that you were in real estate. Is that true?"

"Well, yes, it is," said Brenda. "Why?"

"Do you have about ten acres outside of Oklahoma City for sale?"

"I have a hundred acres outside of Oklahoma City for sale. Why?"

"I've got an idea," said Harry…

Dick was just getting out of the shower when the doorbell to his condo chimed. He answered the door wearing nothing but a towel and was surprised almost to the level of shock when he saw Harry standing in the doorway. Harry was shaven, dressed, and looking fantastic.

"Hey, buddy," said Dick. "I thought you would be in "Hangover Hell" for about a month. You look terrific. What's up?"

"Dicky boy," Harry said with a flourish, "if the Phoenix can rise from the fuckin' ashes, then so can we."

Dick just stared at his friend and thought, *Man, we think way too much alike!*

Chapter Thirty

Some fifteen hundred miles away it was raining in Boston. It was unusually cool as well for late spring. Antonio Fastallo sat in the huge Georgian chair in his study this dreary morning, sipping occasionally on a Café e latte as he carefully perused the pages of the *Herald*. He wore a troubled look on his face as evidenced by the deep furrows on his brow "Joey!" he snapped over the intercom and almost instantly the oversized mahogany pocket doors slid open and his lieutenant was at his side.

"Yes, Don Antonio. How may I be of service to you?"

"I am concerned with what I have read in the papers today. My nephew's place in the Keys has been burned to the ground," the Don explained.

"That is most unfortunate, Don Antonio," Joey responded solemnly.

"Oh, I think that fortune had little to do with it, my loyal friend; and so the paper alludes as well," the Don concluded.

"I see, Don Antonio," Joey replied with a new awareness.

"I am not surprised that Enrico has not contacted me because of his misdirected pride…he is just like his father. But I tell you, Joey, a sin against him is a sin against me, for he is my blood."

"Yes, Don Antonio. It would be my honor to act on your behalf," Joey offered.

"I would like you and Frankie to go down there and sniff the ashes for the scent of the maiale who did this deed." Don Antonio continued, "And, Joey, perhaps he would like to smell his flesh burning, since he likes to play with the matches...capish?"

Joey nodded with understanding and was about to leave when Don Antonio added, "One more thing—keep this between us. It would serve no purpose for my nephew to know about this at this time."

Harry filled Dick in with all that he knew about the fire to date. Dick was shocked to learn about the faithful Jamaican woman who had been murdered. He didn't know her as well as Harry, but it hurt him just the same.

They agreed to take care of all funeral expenses for her and provide her family with a generous check in recognition of her dedicated service. In addition, they would post a $50,000 reward for information leading to an arrest and the conviction of the arsonist.

They also agreed to pay all the employees of the Realm layoff benefits until such time it should cease as a business entity. Dick had already contacted the insurance company and was to meet with them later in the day.

Dick was about to tell Harry about his trip to Oklahoma when the telephone interrupted their conversation. When Dick answered it he was surprised to hear the voice on the other end.

"Dick, this is..."

"Brenda. I'm glad you called...we're making good progress here." Dick failed to notice Harry squirming nervously in his chair as he continued his conversation with her.

"Dick...what is going on with you two?"

"Whaddya mean," he asked.

"Harry called me early this morning and wanted to know about land availability out here in Oklahoma City," she explained.

Dick glanced at Harry who quickly looked away. "You got me on that one, hon," Dick answered.

She went on, "And I was surprised that you confided in him about Rick, before discussing such a sensitive issue as that with me."

Harry rose from his seat and walked to the other side of the room.

Dick then said, "Baby…let me get back to you…bye." Dick laid the phone quietly back on its cradle and said, "Harry…you wanna tell me what in the hell is going on?"

When he didn't answer right away, Dick asked, "How did you know about my son?"

Harry sat back down and answered calmly, "Amber told me."

Harry related his dream of the previous night as Dick tried to make sense out of what he was saying.

"She has come to me before, Dick. I can't explain it…she just seems to be there for me when I really need her. Why do you think I came over here this morning with this 'can do' attitude? It's because of her, Dick. She just comes to me…that's all."

It was Dick's turn to sit down. As incredible as it seemed, Dick believed him. There was no other explanation. How he would explain this to Brenda, he didn't know, but he believed his friend.

"Now, what's this about buying land in Oklahoma?" Dick asked.

"Well, that's what I came over here to talk to you about," Harry explained. "Now, we're just talking, of course, but I was thinking of relocating in the Oklahoma City area and rebuilding our club there…and a hotel, too."

Dick just sat there in stunned silence…he couldn't believe his own ears. Harry rambled on.

"Ya know, Dicky, it would be just like when we were kids in the Army…rock and roll and…"

HARRY JOHN FAULKNER, JR.
DICK SWARTHOUT

"Have you lost your fuckin' mind, Harry?" Dick interrupted. Harry could tell that Dick was pissed, because he seldom cussed at him, or for that matter, raised his voice.

"Here we are…for nearly three hours we've talked and I have yet to hear you express one damn bit of concern about who could have done this shit to us and why! You have no idea that we have only a fifteen-day supply of cash in the business, adjusting for the shutdown's effect on revenue and expenses. Do you think that the insurance company is just going to give us a check this afternoon? And now you want to move us to Tumbleweed City where we can ride bulls and you can sing 'Don't Fence Me In' to a bunch of friggin' yahoos?"

Dick had never been as mad at his friend as he was now. He didn't give Harry a chance to reply. He picked up his briefcase, strode to the door and as he was leaving, turned and said, "Lock the damned door when you leave!"

Harry sat in silence in Dick's condo. He was hurt deeply. His best friend, in all their years together, had never talked to him with such disrespect. He didn't even get a chance to talk to him about his son…the fact that all of them could be back together in the place where they had the most fun in their lives. He didn't care about what they did…he just wanted them together as a family. He was heartbroken.

"Maybe the time has come to go our separate ways," he murmured.

Chapter Thirty-One

Dick stormed out the door and got into his car. He had never been so angry with anybody in his life.

"Fuckin' playboy," he muttered. "All his adult life I've taken care of the sensible side of the problems and all he's ever done was be the fuckin' artist." Dick was beside himself with anger at his friend and he really was at a loss to understand why. He had never sworn at Harry or been that disrespectful to their friendship in all the years they were together. He had always understood Harry's weaknesses and been able to work around them. He never took Harry to task for anything. He just made things work. That was his job. It was what he did.

"Every time there's a God-damned problem I have to solve it," Dick said aloud as he thundered down the road at much too great a speed.

The animal that ran out if front of the car brought Dick back from his tirade. He swerved the car in order to miss the furry thing that loped out in front of his speeding car and all he knew from then on until the car stopped was that he was spinning out of control. The front end finally came to rest against a solid tree. The tree was a foot and a half past the front end and the airbag had opened hitting Dick full in the face leaving him dazed and bruised in the front seat. He was momentarily knocked unconscious and when he awoke he found that his legs were pinned under the steering wheel. He struggled mightily but was hopelessly locked in the grip of the bent and mangled steering wheel. The smell of gasoline was everywhere.

Dick felt an electrical shock on his shin. It was coming from a wire that had been knocked loose in the crash. It kept shorting out against his leg. It didn't really hurt, but it terrified Dick because he knew that it was also emitting a spark every time it touched his leg. *All this gasoline,* he thought. *I am not gonna fuckin' die here!* Dick cursed at the sky. "Not now that I have a son! Not now that I have my Brenda back!" He screamed at the sky and began to cry because he realized at that moment what he was so angry about. He wasn't angry with Harry. He was furious with himself. He hated himself for having missed seventeen years of his son's life. He wanted to be furious with Harry or even Brenda for that matter, but he knew he had no one to blame but himself. He had made his decision so many years ago to throw in with Harry and let their lives take their own course. The fact that he knew nothing about "young Rick," as he had come to calling him, didn't make it the least bit easier. He was screaming now. "I won't fuckin' die here, I won't fuckin' die here, I swear to Christ I won't fuckin' die here!" He passed out.

He awoke. Everything was bright and white. He didn't know where he was. He looked around and realized that he was in bed somewhere. He tried to get up, but as soon as he moved, his head began to pound with a throbbing headache. His memory started to flood back to him. He had visions of spinning out of control, hitting a tree, his airbag hitting him in the face, and that damn wire shocking his leg. The leg still hurt like hell. His eyes fluttered full open and he started to take stock. He couldn't move because he was strapped to the bed. He had a tube in his nose and one in each of his arms into which flowed some sort of liquid from a plastic bag. He had monitors strapped to his vital points to check his heart rate and respiration. He had a headache, a sore stomach and chest, but most of the pain seemed to center on his leg that felt as though it were swollen to twice its size.

He looked around and saw a man in a doctor's smock. "Where the hell am I?" he asked. "And who are you?"

The man in the doctor's smock said, "You're at the Del Ray Medical Center and I am doctor Ivan Puente, the director of this facility."

"How did I get here?" asked Dick.

"You were brought in by helicopter about eleven o'clock this morning. You were found trapped in your car by a passing police cruiser. You're damn lucky, too, because you were in a ditch and couldn't be readily seen from the road. The officer saw some smoke off the road and when he went to investigate, he found you trapped in your vehicle. It's a good thing he found you when he did because the car was beginning to burn because of a spark that kept arcing against a pool of gasoline."

"Oh yeah," said Dick, "I remember that. Is that why my leg is so sore?"

Just then the door to Dick's room opened up and in through the door came an ashen Harry Foster. "Hey, buddy," said Harry, "how you feelin'?"

"I feel okay," returned Dick. "I'm a little banged up, but other than that...I'm in the pink. Hey, listen, Har," said Dick. "I'm really sorry about this morning. I never should have blown up at you like that. I'm really sorry. It's just that..."

Harry interrupted him by saying, "Hey, listen, bud. Don't even think about it. I should have known better than to go off half-cocked without discussing it with you."

"Hey, forget about it. We'll talk about it later."

"Can I do anything for you partner?" asked Harry.

"Yeah, get that doctor Puente in here to give me some pain meds for my leg. It's fuckin' killing me." Dick looked down at where his left leg should have been. It wasn't. The whole bottom half from the knee down was gone.

"Harry!" Dick screamed. "Where's my fuckin' leg? What the fuck did they do to me?"

He was thrashing about the bed when Harry came over to grab Dick by the shoulders. "Easy buddy. It got broken so badly in the car wreck, they had to amputate. I'm sorry, man!"

"You're sorry!" screamed Dick back at Harry. "What the fuck are you sorry about? You got both of your fuckin' legs."

Just then the door opened up and in came Brenda. Dick took one look at her and screamed at Harry with tears streaming down his face. "Get her the fuck outta here. I don't want to see her! Get her out now!"

Chapter Thirty-Two

Dick looked around the hospital room and saw that he was alone. It was daylight, but he could tell that it was raining. He struggled mightily to swing himself into a sitting position on the side of the bed. The amputated leg was on fire and throbbing as he tried to shake the dizziness from his head. He methodically removed the I.V. from his arm and paused another moment to pull himself together. He knew it was now or never. He slowly slid off the bed and supported himself on his good leg. He was shaky, but able to stand as long as he held on to something. He reached for a small chair adjacent to the bed and drew it close. Using it as a modified walker, Dick hobbled his way to the large window of the hospital room. With a great deal of difficulty, he raised the blind to reveal the dreary day. The window was locked and Dick toiled to get it open. He nearly fell as he raised it and the rain began spitting in his face. Still grasping the chair he turned around and with his back now facing the window somehow managed to hoist his torso up onto the sill. He now had his back to the hospital courtyard five stories below.

"God…forgive me," he whispered.

At that very moment the door to his room opened and Brenda entered to witness the unearthly sight of her lover about to commit the unthinkable. She looked into his eyes as he closed them.

"Oh, my God, Dick…no, no!"

Dick tilted his head back and let go of the windowsill. He was plunging backward to his death as Brenda rushed to the precipice.

The impact from the fall shook Dick awake and he was screaming. He opened his eyes to see Brenda over him and saying, "Easy…easy…it's all right…you just had a nightmare…I'm here with you…it's all right."

Dick was soaking wet. He felt awful and was hurting. He needed something for the pain.

"Brenda…please ask them to bring me something."

She rang for the nurse who brought in some meds for the pain.

"Brenda," he said, "can you ever forgive me for my behavior the last time I saw you?"

"Of course, honey…that wasn't you talking…it was someone else," she replied.

"How long have I been here and where in the hell is Harry?"

Brenda told him he'd been in the hospital for five days and that Harry had been in and out checking on him, while trying to keep the business going at the same time.

"You would be proud of your partner for the way he's picked up the slack while you've been here," Brenda advised. "Wait 'til I tell you the…" she stopped talking as she could see Dick wasn't hearing her.

Dick had suddenly remembered that he was missing a lower leg and was trying to come to grips with it. "I can't and won't ask you to have anything to do with a gimp like me, Brenda," he blurted.

"My precious darling, Dick. Don't you know that I love you so much that as long as you are breathing, there could never be anyone else for me?"

Dick looked away, trying to hold back the tears.

Brenda continued to speak, trying to encourage Dick. "The doctor said that they have some amazing prosthetics out the market these days. With rehab and practice, no one will be able to tell you are missing any part of your leg," she concluded.

"Where's Rick?" Dick asked.

"Oh, he's back in Oklahoma playing baseball and staying with some friends," she said. "He's quite the ball player, you know. His high school team made the state playoffs."

Dick smiled and momentarily forgot about the pity he had for himself. He'd almost forgotten about his own son.

"Brenda...how can anything ever be the same? What the hell good am I to him, you, or anybody else in the world for that matter?" Dick lamented.

Brenda was about to answer when the doctor entered the room.

"Well, Mr. Stuart. It's about time that we get you started on rehab," he stated. "How are you feeling?"

Dick proceeded to tell him about his woes and how depressed he was. The doctor listened patiently and advised Dick that was exactly how he had expected him to feel about his present situation, and that he wasn't much different from other patients.

"However," he added, "it's time for you to stop feeling sorry for yourself, accept what has happened, and move on."

This angered Dick somewhat and the doctor, sensing it, said, "It's okay to get mad. That's the first step to a successful recovery. Sooo...rehab begins at 9:30 sharp in the morning." Doctor Puente left.

Dick, determined to get off the subject of his missing body part said, "Brenda...I don't want you to think that I'm not grateful for you coming to see me, but..."

She cut him off, saying, "There is another reason that I'm here, Dick."

"Oh?" Dick replied.

"Harry has hired me temporarily as a consultant. I said yes because it gives me a chance to be with you for a while," she explained.

Dick was taken aback. "A consultant?" he quizzed.

"Yes," she said. "I'm helping you and Harry with the transition to a point where you are up and running. "For example," she continued, "I met with your insurance company the day before yesterday concerning the claim. You probably were aware that there will be at least a sixty day moratorium on payment of any claim due to the fact there is arson involved," Brenda advised.

Dick knew this, as it was in the policy, but had hoped to work out a low interest loan against the claim proceeds for working capital. Brenda was apparently reading his mind when she mentioned that she had attempted to do the very same thing, but the insurance company declined.

"So, Harry and I approached a major bank in Miami and secured a line of credit of $500,000 and pledged the real estate as collateral. We now have some breathing room without the need to tie up any of yours or Harry's personal assets."

Dick, at that moment, was so very proud of Brenda and his eyes glowed with admiration of her.

"What?" she asked, as she blushed ever so slightly.

"My compliments to you and my friend. It appears he made a good personnel move when he hired you."

"I have something else to tell you, but I think I'll wait until Harry gets here," Brenda teased.

"Oh…I almost forgot to tell you something else that developed during your stay here," she stated. "Harry said that the police arson squad found two charred video cameras in the ashes of the fire. Apparently, there's a…"

Dick shouted, interrupting her, "Yes, yes, yes!!! Those damned cameras in the fire resistant boxes. Why didn't I think of that before? They only found two? We had seven of them in the club," Dick questioned.

Brenda replied that she didn't know about that, but that the local police were going to ask the FBI to look at the film and see if anything could be garnered as a result.

Dick was thinking to himself, "Wow…a lead on this shit already…what a break!" That thought vanished abruptly when Harry Foster, Jr. entered Dick's room with what appeared to be a large roll of blueprints under is arm and triumphantly announced, "Sir Richard, it's time to get off your ass and out of bed. We have an empire to rebuild!!!"

Chapter Thirty-Three

The Firestarter was not happy. He had burned the Realm down to the ground, and still he had not beaten the man that he had made the focus of hatred so strong that it knew no bounds. He knew that Harry Foster had no idea who he was. He also knew that if he discovered his real identity he would still have no reason to fear him.

His hatred was not actually directed at Harry Foster for anything that Harry was guilty of. The anger, in fact, was directed at Antonio Fastallo. The man who was the Boss of Bosses in the mafia family of Boston was the reason that Harry Foster, who used to be Enrico Fastallo, was the focus of the Firestarter's rage.

The Firestarter's name was Jack Ricco and he was on the fast track to be the business agent of the Boston Teamsters. He had the existing president on his side and it looked like he was, as was said in Boston, a lead pipe cinch.

The president, Joe Murphy, wanted one of the "no show" jobs for one of his nephews. Jack Ricco was to put all of his political capital on the line to get Murphy's guy the title of Health and Welfare Administrator and in return Joe Murphy would see to it that Jack was elected to the Business Agent's job.

It all might have worked out except for two serious miscalculations made by Jack Ricco and Tommy Ryan. They thought that because they had the support of the president, they couldn't lose. They also made no bones about what would happen to any local guy who was found to be voting against the "Presidents Choice." Tommy Ryan assumed that as the nephew of the president he couldn't lose. He was wrong.

152

Antonio Fastallo had an interest in the job himself. He wanted to see to it that one of his people was installed in the position. The Teamsters Union was a "money store" in those days and whoever controlled the Health and Welfare funds also had millions available to do with as they pleased.

Antonio Fastallo was accustomed to getting what he wanted. He used an associate by the name of Kevin Feeney. Feeney was a local guy who had a strong connection with all of the line workers. He was clever enough to keep his affiliation with the Fastallo crime family to himself. He was also gifted with the ability to get the rank and file to listen to his point of view. He did it quietly and without threats of any kind. It was the kind of approach that worked with the hard working local drivers. He would cajole and prod the local guy by using his first name and asking after his kids.

"Hey, Joey!" he would holler across the bar. "How's the missus? I hear your boy had a great game against Southie last week. If the man was on the other side he would say, "Hey, Frankie, I hear your boy had a great game against Charles Town last week."

He was the consummate politician and probably could have been elected to any position in the union if he so chose. He chose to stay behind the scenes. He knew that he could be second banana for his whole life and do very well. He chose to let others salve their egos and become the elected officials. They came and they went, but Kevin Feeney was always there to support the winner. It was Boston politics at its finest. Kevin Feeney was a master at it.

The vote to install Tommy Ryan was to come on the second Saturday of the month. It was to be accomplished by the three-member E-Board with no resistance. Joe Murphy believed that he had all three members of the board on his side in order to deliver the job to his nephew.

He was wrong.

Kevin Feeney, who had a long-standing relationship with the sitting Business Agent, James Shanahan, had lobbied long and hard to get the business agent to go against Tommy Ryan.

"Hey, Shaney," he had said. "If you vote for this guy, the next thing that's gonna happen is they're gonna come after you."

"Why do you say that?" Jim Shaney asked.

"Because the promise that's been made to Jackie Ricco for delivering the job to Tommy is to take your job away from you," returned Kevin.

"What's to say that if I vote against Murphy's guy, they won't come after me anyway?"

"They will," answered Kevin, "but they won't get you."

"How can you be so sure of that?" asked the worried Business Agent.

"Shaney," said Feeney, "have I ever failed? Have I ever failed to deliver a vote for you on anything you ever came to me for?"

No, you haven't," said the nervous business agent, "but if you do fail, then I'm out in the street."

"If I do fail," said Kevin, "then we'll both be out in the street." He added, "If you vote with me, Shaney, then at least you have a chance to save your job. If you vote with them, then you will most assuredly lose your position."

Shaney thought about all of the benefits that came from being the Teamster's Business Agent. He thought about the drivers, the expense accounts, and in general, the prestige of the position. He agreed with Kevin Feeney's logic and decided that, in fact, he would stand with Kevin. He had no idea that the force behind Kevin Feeney was Antonio Fastallo. The fact of the matter was that if he did know, he still would have voted with Kevin Feeney on this one.

The vote was cast and true to his word, James Shanahan voted against Joe Murphy's nephew. Joe was furious and vowed to take his revenge out on Shaney by mounting a candidate to defeat him on the next election. The next election was due in eight months.

The election was very much in doubt on the night of the voting. It was generally believed that it was Kevin Feeney's impassioned speech from the Union Hall floor that tipped the scales in Jimmy Shaney's favor.

He started out very slowly. "Gentlemen," said Feeney, "you all know me and you know that when it's all said and done, I stand with the rank and file. If I didn't think that Jimmy Shaney was the guy for the job, I wouldn't be standing in front of you. When did any of you ever reach out for help from Shaney and not get it? When is the last time Jimmy Shaney didn't stand up for you on any grievance with any company at any time? When is the last time you called Jimmy Shaney and he didn't return your call?" Kevin was on a roll now.

"On the other hand, when was the last time you saw President Murphy at any union hall? When was the last time President Murphy ever returned one of your calls?" Feeney could see that he was winning his argument with the men gathered in the union hall. "If you can't get your president to return your calls, why should any of us believe that his lackey would do any better?"

From the back of the hall came a shout. "I don't have to hear any more, Kevin. I'm ready to vote now." It was shouted out by one of the long-standing members of the union who was skillfully placed in the audience to put the last nail in the coffin of Jack Ricco's dream of becoming a big time player in the Teamsters of Boston.

The vote was a landslide. Jimmy Shaney won re-election, and Kevin Feeney won the undying hatred of Jackie Ricco.

Kevin Feeney tasted that hatred the night after the election. He was ambushed outside his home by five of Ricco's thugs and put in the hospital for six weeks of recovery. If Jack Ricco had had any knowledge of the relationship between Kevin Feeney and Don Antonio Fastallo he never would have allowed the ambush to take place.

In less than one year, all five of the attackers had tasted the revenge of Don Fastallo. Two were dead and the other three were maimed in one way or another for life. As a final insult to the five, all five of their homes were burned down.

While Don Fastallo could be the most generous of friends, he was the most vicious of enemies. He wanted to be sure that any man who angered him understood how complete his punishment could be. It wasn't enough to just hurt his enemies physically, he wanted to make sure they were hurt emotionally as well.

"If you take a man's home, you take away his self respect as well."

Jack Ricco knew his time was coming. He had long since discovered his error. The fact that he didn't know that Kevin Feeney was connected to the

155

Don would be of little help. He knew that when it was his turn, the punishment would be swift and perhaps permanent. He left town for Florida. With the aid of a less than honorable plastic surgeon, he changed his face and his name. He was now Benny Meyers. He was also Harry Foster's driver.

He had learned through some of his old connections back home in Boston that Harry Foster was Enrico Fastallo. He was the nephew of the Don himself. It was after learning this little bit of information that his plan for revenge began to take shape. He knew that he could hurt the Don most severely by hurting someone the Don loved.

So far his revenge on Don Fastallo was delicious. He had caused the death of Harry Foster's fiancé, he had burned the Realm down to the ground, and now Harry's best friend was in the hospital with an amputated leg. He was so delighted with himself that he was planning another one of his multiple nights with the hookers of Miami. He was unaware that he had gone completely mad.

"Benny," said Harry, "I need for you to drive Alisha to the airport. I'm having Brenda's son flown in for a surprise and I would like somebody to meet him at the airport. I can't go because of a meeting I have today at police headquarters. We are going to be looking at the tapes from the security cameras to see if we can get a line on the prick that started this fire. I don't really care about the fire, but I really want him for what he did to Moesha."

Benny was beside himself with anticipation. He couldn't believe his luck. He was going to have the new love of Harry Foster's life and his best friend's son all to himself to do as he wished. Maybe he wouldn't need to go to Miami tonight. Maybe he would take his evil passions out on Alisha.

Chapter Thirty-Four

"Good morning, Alisha,," said Benny. "Nice day for a drive to the airport."

Benny could hardly contain himself. He would make Don Antonio Fastallo pay big time today. He would strike him where it hurt the most… in his family. All he had to do was stay in control for another two hours and he would have Alisha and Dick's son Rick in the limousine to do with as he pleased. The thought of the cruelty he intended to heap upon the boy was almost as exciting as the sexual depravities he had planned for Alisha. He intended to abuse both the boy and the beautiful Alisha before he killed them. He felt a slight pang of remorse over Alisha's upcoming death. Not because of any compassion, but because of that sweet body she possessed. He could feel himself becoming aroused just thinking about it.

"This could be quite a day," said Alisha. "Harry is going to the police station to check the video tapes from the security cameras and maybe find out who burned the Realm down. I hope so. I get upset every time I think about it and remember what happened to Moesha. I just don't know how someone could do a thing like that," she said finally.

"I don't know," said Benny. "Sometimes you just don't know about the evil that can lurk in some people's hearts." He said this almost to himself and Alisha thought it seemed quite strange, but let it pass. She had no reason not to.

They arrived at the airport with just fifteen minutes before young Rick's plane was to land at Miami International Airport. Benny expertly pulled the car to a stop at the curb and Alisha said, "I'll jump out and meet Rick and you can just wait here, Benny. That way we don't have to park the limo and we can get back on the road more quickly when he lands."

Benny agreed by saying, "I'll be right here waiting for you when you come out."

With that Alisha jumped out of the limo and walked inside. Benny watched a cop admire Alisha as she walked through the doors to the terminal and thought to himself, *Fuck you, cop. I'll be fuckin' her in about an hour and a half while you're still standing here like the redneck asshole you are.*

Alisha was excited as she headed for the gate. She knew what a terrific guy Dick was and she couldn't have been happier for him that he had found his son. *If he is anything like his dad,* she thought, *he should be a great kid.*

She had had the opportunity to talk to Dick about his boy over the past few days during visits to the hospital. Dick spoke of him with pride and something that was close to reverence. He couldn't believe that he had a son.

He would be a great dad to this boy, she thought to herself as she watched the jumbo jet roll up to the gate.

She was holding a sign with Rick's name on it when she started to laugh out loud. Through the gate came Dick Stuart. A seventeen-year-old Dick Stuart maybe, but it was Dick Stuart coming through the gate. She knew she had to be careful because Rick still didn't know anything about Dick being his dad. She held up the sign so the boy could see it and acted as though she were surprised when he walked up to her.

"Hi, I'm Rick Mcleod. Are you here to pick me up?" Alisha said that indeed she was and that she had a car waiting outside for them.

Benny saw them coming. "Now you'll pay, Fastallo, you son-of-a-bitch," he said aloud as they approached the car. He intended to hurt both of these people before he killed them and then go back to his local plastic surgeon and disappear again. He was beside himself with joy. He was finally going to inflict a wound on Fastallo that would hurt him more than if he actually had gotten to shoot him in the head the way he so desperately wanted to.

"Maybe some day," he said aloud and began to giggle like the madman he had become.

"Rick, this is Benny," she said. Rick sort of mumbled a greeting the way seventeen-year-old boys do and said that he was pleased to meet him.

You won't be for long, you little asshole, Benny thought to himself. When they left the airport, Benny took a turn that would lead them directly away from home.

"Benny," said Alisha, "where are you going?" There was no alarm in Alisha's voice, only curiosity. Benny didn't answer. She asked again.

"Benny, are we going somewhere before we go home?"

"Shut the fuck up," said Benny with such malice that it caused Alisha to sit bolt upright in her seat and demand where they were going.

"Benny, what the hell are you doing and where are we going?" she demanded.

Young Rick was sitting in the back seat with Alisha, totally confused, but didn't dare open his mouth.

It was then that Alisha noticed that the doors were locked from the driver's compartment controls and the door handles had been removed from both doors in the passengers' seats. Although Alisha was stunned by this, all she could do was stare at the back of Benny's head and in an instant she knew who had burned the Realm to the ground and who was responsible for Moesha's death. She looked at this beautiful boy beside her and she was terrified for both of them...

"It was you," she said.

Chapter Thirty-Five

Harry was walking up to the police station. He was to find a Lieutenant Cobb in order to view the security tapes from the night of the fire. Lieutenant Cobb was very impatient. He had tried to do it sooner, but the liability and admissibility of evidence found without Harry's presence made that impossible.

Harry hoped that he would find what he was looking for on the tapes because he so dearly wanted to find the son-of-a-bitch who had murdered Moesha. He was upset about the fire, but knew that the insurance would take care of that problem, and nothing could bring back Moesha.

The anger that he felt was something a bit foreign to Harry. He knew that it probably came from somewhere deep in his genetic make up. He was surprised at it, but he didn't mind the feeling. He felt that if anybody could hurt another person the way, whoever it was, had hurt Moesha, then that person deserved to be hurt as well. He would have been perfectly happy to inflict the punishment himself.

The police station was a low one level stucco building that had been painted beige. It had palm trees around it and the only thing that gave its true purpose away was the blue and white sign announcing "Police." Inside there was a raised desk behind a bulletproof glass. A burly police sergeant was sitting behind the desk. He was big and had a ruddy complexion. He had an intimidating look about him that was contradicted by the rather delicate wire rim glasses that hung on his nose. He would look over the glasses whenever he spoke to anyone. His hair was red, his eyes were blue, and the name-tag on his short-sleeved shirt said "Sergeant Kelly."

"Yes, sir," said the sergeant. "May I help you with something?" The question sounded more like "Waddya want and waddya doin' here anyway?"

Sergeant Kelly just didn't trust anybody that wasn't a cop.

"My name is Harry Foster and I'm here to see Lieutenant Cobb about some video tapes."

"Oh, yeah, Mr. Foster. He's been expecting you." The burly sergeant's attitude changed when he realized who he was talking to because he was fully aware of the trouble the fire at the Realm had caused in this man's life. He punched an intercom key and said, "Hey, Loo, Mr. Foster's here to see you."

"I'll be right out," Harry heard through the bulletproof glass.

In about five minutes a giant of a man came into the foyer. He was about six foot four, black and looked as though he had been cut from black granite. Everything about the man warned of danger except his eyes. Harry had seen eyes that soft only on a deer.

"Hello, Mr. Foster," said the giant. "I'm Lieutenant Cory Cobb. I'm glad you could come down this morning."

"I'm glad to come down to help, Lieutenant," said Harry. "I want this guy so bad I can taste it," he added.

"Well, then let's get right to it. We have been able to narrow it down to about two hours of tape, so it shouldn't take us too long."

"Did you see anything on the tapes yet?" asked Harry.

"No, not really," said the lieutenant.

Harry had no idea that Lieutenant Cobb didn't need to see the tapes. He had no idea that Uncle Tony had already placed a call to Lieutenant Cobb the night before.

The lieutenant led Harry down a long corridor into a darkened room that held a VCR and a 25-inch television. Harry couldn't wait to get to work although he did have a disquieting feeling that he might not like what he saw on the tapes.

They isolated on the Jamaica Room where Moesha was found. They both agreed that if the perpetrator were to be seen on tape, this would be the tape he was on.

It was very disturbing to watch Moesha going about her business of closing down the Jamaica Room. At 02:45 a.m., by the tape's counter, a figure moved into the frame.

Moesha looked up and didn't seem to be the least bit disturbed by the person's arrival. It seemed to Harry that she even smiled at the man.

The man walked up to Moesha and hit her with the full force of a punch straight into her jaw. She collapsed to the floor from the strength of the blow and the man was immediately upon her with a roll of duct tape, binding both her hands and feet. His back was still to the camera and Harry hadn't yet recognized the assailant. The man turned to wrestle Moesha into the chair that would be her death trap that night.

Harry's heart stopped cold. "Lieutenant Cobb, we have to get to the airport right now. That man is my driver Benny Myers, and he has my fiancé and my best friend's son with him. If we don't find him right now..."

Chapter Thirty-Six

Alisha could do nothing but sit back and wonder and worry. She had no idea what was going on or why. She just knew that she was in great trouble. The man driving the limousine, a man she thought she knew, had seemingly gone mad. He had been mumbling for the past half hour about his friends being hurt and now it was Fastallo's turn.

Who the hell is Fastallo? Alisha thought to herself. *And what does he have to do with me?*

Then she remembered the opening night of the Realm and the table of men that Harry had paid so much attention to. She also remembered that man who had given her son Tommy so much trouble. She remembered one of the other girls, a girl who had come down from Boston, saying that the man's name was Antonio Fastallo and that he was a gangster or something. She reasoned that if this abduction had anything to do with Antonio Fastallo then she really was frightened and was at a loss as to what to do about her situation.

Benny was careful not to drive too fast or too slow. He did nothing to attract attention to the limousine. It wouldn't do to be stopped by a dumb cop at this point. Not when he was so close to getting even with Fastallo.

He was driving to a secluded spot that he knew of out in the countryside. It was just an old house with a big barn attached to it down a back road, but it would serve his purposes very well. He intended to take the full day with these two people in back and he didn't want somebody just happening to drive by and see the limousine.

He would drive in the barn, and take these two inside. It would be impossible to see the limousine from the road and he had no intention of using any lights. He intended for both of them to be dead before there was any need to turn on any lamps.

He had no idea that he had just made the mistake of his life. He had no idea that the Don already knew about his face change and the fact that he was living in Florida. He had no idea that the doctor he had gone to for his plastic surgery was the same doctor used by all the organized crime people who needed to change the way they looked. He had no idea that his doctor, one of the finest in South Florida, had graduated from the Boston University Medical Program and then had gone on to specialize in Reconstructive Surgery. He had no idea that Don Antonio Fastallo had paid for all of it.

Barry Gold was a world-class medical student. He had maxed all of his exams and was on the fast track to being whatever he wanted to be in the field of medicine.

He had decided on the field of Reconstructive Surgery. It was a field that offered the potential of enormous profits and rarely did the practitioner have to deal with life and death situations.

Barry had decided on this particular field of medicine, not from a concern for his fellow man, but for his love of lots of money. He knew that one of the fastest ways to make lots of money was to appeal to the egos of aging, frightened, and very rich people. He was very clever and he was very cunning. He was also in very big trouble.

He was sitting in the back seat of a Boston police car with his hands cuffed behind his back. He had been arrested for trying to sell a quantity of cocaine to an undercover cop in Kenmore Square. A very beautiful undercover cop named Patty Murphy. Officer Murphy had worked Barry beautifully with both her brain and her body. She had become very fond of Barry and hated to take him down on the drug charges. They had been dating for the past six months and Barry had fallen in love with Patty and in spite of the rules, Patty had fallen in love with Barry.

The BPD didn't really want Barry, but they were trying to use him to get to whomever it was that was supplying him his drugs. They wanted to get to "Mr. Big."

Patty knew that if Barry was the reason that "Mr. Big" whoever he was, went down, Barry would be in great danger. Patty didn't want this. She called a halt to the investigation claiming that she could no longer deal with it and she had convinced her superiors that Barry was never going to make a mistake and give up his source. Not to her. Not to anybody. Her commanding officer didn't buy her story but he said, "Bring him in and book him."

Patty knew that she hadn't fooled her boss and she was grateful that he understood. She knew that she hadn't fooled him when he said, "Officer Murphy, I don't see any reason why you should arrest this guy. I think we'll let some of the other officers get him. We may need you undercover again and I don't want to blow your cover."

She knew she would never work undercover again. It was one thing for her boss to cut her some slack for having fallen in love with someone she was investigating, but she knew that he would look at it as proof positive that she didn't have what it took to be an undercover cop. He was probably right.

Barry's mind was racing. He knew that if he were convicted that it would be the end of his career. He knew he had to get these charges squashed or his dream of becoming a wealthy doctor would be smashed like a small boat upon the rocks. It was here that fate intervened.

He was going to be rich someday, but for now he was dirt poor and couldn't pay for a lawyer. He was appointed one. His name was Danny Macero and he was raised in the North End of Boston and he knew the Fastallo family very well. It was these connections that would create a long-standing relationship between the Don and the aspiring doctor.

"Don Fastallo," began the lawyer. "I have just been given a new client who cannot pay his bills. The courts assigned him to me and his story is very interesting."

"How is that, my friend?" asked the Don.

"He is a medical student," replied the attorney.

"How is that of interest to me?" the Don asked again.

"It is his specialty that may interest you, and the position he finds himself in," said Macero. "He is to be a plastic surgeon, or a specialist in reconstructive surgery as it is called today. I think that the Don might be able to use such a man if he could put him in his debt."

The Don sat back for a moment and thought about the suggestion. After a time he said, "What is he charged with?"

"Possession with intent to distribute," answered the lawyer.

"What's this 'gonna-be-a-surgeon's' name?" asked the Don.

"Barry Gold," said the attorney.

The Don was aware of a medical student that one of his people had told him about a while ago. He had borrowed some money from one of the loan sharks in the Don's organization and was attempting to pay it back by selling cocaine and "speed" to his fellow classmates. The students would use them regularly, both for recreation and to try and keep awake during exam times. He sold quite a bit of goods and took no money other than a pay down on the thousands of dollars the loan shark had given him towards tuition.

The Don also knew that he was at the top of his class and was considered the most likely to succeed by all of his classmates and his professors. The Don made no commitment, but said, "How much is his bail?"

"Fifty thousand dollars," said Macero.

"I will arrange his bail and I want you to bring him to me." Then the Don said, "Now if you'll excuse me, I have other work to attend to."

Attorney Macero, understanding that he was being dismissed, excused himself by saying, "Thank you for your time, Don Fastallo. I will have Doctor Gold in your office by noon tomorrow."

"That'll be fine," said the Don. Macero heard the door to the Don's office opening and in the doorway stood Tony. Tony's presence meant that the meeting was over and it was time for whomever the Don was talking with to leave. The attorney did just that.

"How did you get me out?" asked the befuddled Barry Gold.

"I didn't get you out, Barry. Your employer did."

"My employer?" asked Barry. "Who would that be?"

"Look, Barry, I'm a lawyer. I don't give a shit what you do for a living, but stop with the innocent bullshit! I have taken an oath to help my clients in all of their legal battles. I'm doing just that. I know you've been dealing coke and I know who your supplier is."

Barry sat back in the cab and wondered what would be happening next. He couldn't imagine that Jimmy Cavallo, his source for cocaine, would spring for the five thousand necessary to put down on a fifty thousand dollar bail to get him out.

The cab pulled up in front of the Italian-American club on Medford Street in Somerville and confused him even more. The Somerville Italian-American Club was nothing more than a storefront. The windows were covered so that no one from the street could see inside. In order to get inside the door, you had to be known by the man sitting on a stool just inside the doorway. He was the guard.

He would be at the door every time Don Antonio Fastallo was at the club. He was always big and he was always without a sense of humor if you were a stranger. The big man greeted Danny Macero with easy familiarity, but he eyed Barry with great suspicion.

"Hey, Danny," said the man. "How ya doin'?" He looked menacingly at Barry and said, "Hey, who's this guy, Danny?" There was a smile on his face, but it had a malevolence to it that took Barry Gold by surprise. He didn't know this man, but he knew that he would never want him angry with him.

"Hey, Billy," said Danny. "This is Barry Gold. He's a friend of mine and he has an appointment to see Mr. Fastallo."

Mr. Fastallo? thought Barry. Who the hell is Mr. Fastallo? The name sounded familiar, but Barry couldn't pull it out of his memory bank.

Billy picked up the phone that was seated on a table by the door and said, "Hey, Tony, Danny Macero is here with a guy named Barry Gold. He says he has an appointment with the boss."

Big Billy listened to what was being said at the other end of the line. He hung up the phone and said to Barry, "Nice to meet you. Go on in, the boss is waiting for you."

"Yeah, you, too," mumbled Barry and was relieved when Billy let them pass.

They walked into what Barry expected to be a back room. He was unprepared for what he saw. In the back of this "storefront" was a magnificent office. It would have been worthy of any executive of any major company in the world. The exception to this was the fact that it had absolutely no windows. Instead of windows, it had a bank of television monitors that scanned the building outside for 360 degrees. It was possible to see who or what was at anyplace around the building at any time. No one could possibly get into the area without being seen.

That's elaborate, thought Barry, and then it hit him. Mr. Fastallo! Don Antonio Fastallo? Oh, shit, Barry, he thought to himself. What the hell are you into now?

Tony had led them into the office and seated them in the heavy leather chairs that surrounded the dark mahogany desk. He offered them coffee, which they both declined, and said, "Mr. Fastallo will be with you in a moment."

Jesus, Barry thought to himself, this guy's bigger than the one at the front door! Tony had left them alone and Barry said to Danny, "Jesus Christ, Danny. Don't they have any small guys working here?"

They almost jumped out of their skins when a secret panel in the wall, that hid a small bathroom, opened and out came the Don himself.

"Just me," said the Don. "I always feel more comfortable surrounded by guys that are at least the size of a small train. It discourages people from just walking up to me to talk. I sort of like my privacy."

It was all said with tongue in cheek. Danny laughed and Barry squirmed a bit. He was afraid that he might be in over his head.

"I understand that you are a talented doctor," the Don began with no preamble.

"I suppose so," answered Barry wondering how this man knew about his medical skills. "I try, anyway," he added.

"You do more than try, according to your professors and all your professional colleagues."

Barry had never dealt with anybody in this world of organized crime, but he was smart enough to keep his mouth shut and listen.

"I understand that you have done some work for a friend of mine. A Mister Jimmy Cavallo?"

Barry said nothing.

"I also understand that you owe this friend of mine a fair amount of money?"

Barry still said nothing and the Don admired that. He had seen many a man start to stutter and stammer at this point in the conversation. He knew that his presence and his position intimidated most people. It didn't seem to bother this doctor. The Don was beginning to feel more comfortable with the decision he was about to make.

"Do you know who I am?" asked the Don.

"Yes, I do, Don Antonio Fastallo," answered Barry.

The question surprised Danny Macero, but the answer from Barry left him thunderstruck. The answer pleased the Don very much and he was now very comfortable with the decision that he was making. He could tell that this young man not only had a brain in his head, but he knew about showing the proper respect. He had used the term "Don." He had used it and he seemed perfectly comfortable with it. He didn't seem to be the least bit intimidated by the Don, but he did seem to respect him.

"I have a proposition for you, Doctor Gold. I understand that you are about to specialize in reconstructive surgery."

170

Barry still hadn't said a word, but merely nodded his head.

"In my business, Doctor Gold, we sometimes have a need for people to 'disappear'."

This caused Barry a certain discomfort.

The Don, seeing his face, chuckled a bit and said, "Come, come, Doctor. Not, that kind of disappear. I mean sometimes they have to go away because they might be in danger from the law or from somebody outside the law that they may have made angry. It would be very beneficial to me if the services of a fine reconstructive surgeon were available to me."

Barry was finally beginning to see where this conversation was going, but with all the cunning that was some where in his genetic make-up, he still said nothing.

The Don continued, "If I found such a surgeon, I would be willing to make any problems he might have at this time to go away."

Still Barry said nothing.

"I might even find a way to forgive a substantial debt that doctor owed to me."

Barry said nothing.

The Don started to laugh and said, "Okay, okay. I could probably pay his expenses while he learned this specialty of his!"

The Don was pleased and amused at the brashness and boldness of this young doctor. He must have some Italian blood in him to be so clever, the Don thought to himself.

"The only thing that I will insist on, Dr. Gold, is that I am informed of every surgery you do on people that I might be interested in. Other than that, you are free to pursue your career without interference from me."

The Don then sat back in his enormous chair and looked at this doctor that he had just offered to make a significant investment in. It was his turn to say nothing.

His shoulders had barely touched the back of his chair when, Barry finally said, "Don Fastallo, if you had forced me to answer just after saying that you could make this trouble I have right now go away, I would have agreed to your terms. I most certainly agree with your terms as they exist now!"

It was some years later when Don Fastallo received a call from Doctor Gold in Florida that a certain Jack Ricco from Boston was seeking his services. The Don thanked the doctor and then made a decision that he was about to curse himself for. He decided to leave Jack alone and let him go on with his life.

The Don had just heard of Alisha's kidnapping from a phone call he had received from Tony down in Florida.

"Boss," said Tony. "Harry's fiancé and his partner's son have been kidnapped by someone."

It was at that moment that the Don knew who had burned down the Realm, who was responsible for that girl's death, and who it was that had just kidnapped Alisha and Rick.

"Jack Ricco, you little prick," the Don hissed into the phone.

"Reach out for all of our people down there, Tony," the Don said. "Find this little pig and kill him! Call that Lieutenant Cobb and ask him to call me. I want to know everything that is going on and when we find this little bastard I don't want it handled in the courts!"

Tony had heard this kind of malevolence in the Don's voice on only a few occasions. The Don was usually businesslike in any instruction he may have had to give Tony. It didn't make any difference if he was sending him out to lease a new car or if he was instructing him to remove a wayward associate with terrible malice. It was business.

This, Joey knew, was personal…

Chapter Thirty-Seven

Lieutenant Cory Cobb had just hung up the receiver of his phone. He had just received a call from Don Antonio Fastallo in Boston. He now knew how serious this kidnapping had become. He intended to solve this one because he felt that he owed the Don. He owed him for some help he had received on a murder case some years ago.

It was the murder of three young black women. It was a senseless murder and it infuriated the young Officer Cobb. One of the victims was his niece. The case had generated tremendous publicity because it was particularly gruesome in nature, and the fact that all three of the young women had been raped made the case that much more titillating. He had received a call in the middle of the night.

"Officer Cobb?" the voice asked. Still asleep, the call had made Cory Cobb less than polite.

"Yeah, who the fuck is this and what are you doin' callin' me at this early motherfuckin' hour?"

"My name is Tony Fastallo. I'm calling you from Boston."

"Yeah, so?"

"I know that you have a difficult case on your hands and I would like to help you solve it."

Officer Cobb was becoming interested because if this call was from Boston and if this man really was Tony Fastallo, or Don Antonio Fastallo, as he was written up in the papers, then he might really be able to help him solve the case.

"We think that you are looking for a man named William Sawyer. His name used to be Arthur Shannon and he is wanted up here for a series of gangland murders, and he is also a suspect in a number of rapes and assaults. All of the rapes and assaults were committed against black women. He has changed his name and he has had plastic surgery to change his appearance. Go see a Dr. Barry Gold and he can give you a picture of the man as he looks today. If you find this man, then you find your murderer."

Cory Cobb, fully awake now, said, "Why are you telling me about this guy and why do you want him off the streets?"

"My reasons," said the caller, "are just that. My reasons. If you don't want the information, then just ignore the call. If you find this man and make the arrest your name will be instantly famous for awhile and it could help you career."

The phone line went dead.

Officer Cory Cobb decided that he would take that phone call seriously and found William Sawyer. He found him, then he booked him, then he sent him to trial, and he was there when they sent him to prison to await his execution on three counts of 1st degree murder.

On the day William Sawyer was executed, Officer Cobb became Lieutenant Cobb.

He had just received another phone call from Antonio Fastallo.

"Lieutenant Cobb, my old friend, I think I have a way for you to earn your captain's bars."

Cory had recognized the man's voice instantly. It had been a number of years, but time had done nothing diminish the importance of this man's voice in Cory Cobb's life.

"You're looking for a man named Benny Myers this time. As before, go to Dr. Barry Gold. He will be able to provide you with a current picture of Mr. Meyers as he looks today. Find him and you find the kidnapper of Harry Foster's fiancé and Dick Stuart's son. I have business with this man and I would appreciate it if we could have some time with him before you arrest him."

Lieutenant Cory Cobb had the sense that this wasn't really a request. It was expected.

Cory Cobb said, "No problem, Don Antonio." He felt no remorse for having made the decision to turn over this Benny Meyers to Antonio Fastallo and his family.

Yeah, I owe, thought Cory Cobb to himself...

Chapter Thirty-Eight

Benny had already taped young Rick to a chair. He had used duct tape to tape his hands behind his back and to tape each leg to a leg of the chair. Rick could not move. He decided not to tape his mouth or his eyes because he wanted Alisha's pain and shame to be made even worse by making sure that young Rick saw what he was doing to her. He intended to do delicious things to her. Well, at least he thought, so and it made him giggle again in his mad way.

"What are you doing?" said Rick. He was obviously terrified, but he couldn't be quiet. "Leave her alone!" he hollered.

Benny stopped toying with Alisha's hair and turned to young Rick. He stood in front of him and slapped him hard in the face. The boy's eyes started to tear from the sharp blow, but he sat staunchly defiant, staring at Benny.

"You know, you really are an asshole, mister!" Rick shouted at Benny.

Benny slapped him again and caused Rick's head to snap back.

"Fuck you, mister!"

Rick had never spoken to an adult in such a way in his life but he didn't care. *This man is an asshole!* Rick thought.

Benny closed his fist this time and punched the boy square in the face causing blood to spurt from his nose. The boy lost consciousness.

When Rick lost consciousness, Benny decided that he wasn't worth the trouble of listening to and taped his mouth shut. "Shut the fuck up, you little brat!" said Benny.

It was now time to pay attention to Alisha.

She is a beautiful little thing, he thought. *I am gonna have so much fun with this little bitch.*

Alisha's eyes were wide with terror. She could no longer hide her fear. When she saw what Benny had just done to Rick, she knew her fate was to be no better.

From out of his pocket he pulled out a knife. He had never been without a knife since the day he swore vengeance on Antonio Fastallo. He was never without a knife and he was never without a Zippo lighter. He loved to cut things up and he loved to burn things down. He was going to do both of those things today. "But first some fun," he said out loud.

He came to Alisha with the knife blade. She squirmed as he placed the knife blade against her chest. He put the sharpened blade against the top button of her shirt. With a flick, the button was cut from the shirt. Then he moved to the next button down and repeated the procedure until her shirt fell open exposing her breasts. She was wearing a lacey see-through bra and the sight of her nipples through the thin material caused Benny's eyes to shine. His breathing had become ragged as he reached and took one of her nipples between his thumb and forefinger. He twisted the nipple as though he was twisting a cap off a bottle and it hurt Alisha enough to cause her to cry out in pain. This made Benny even more excited. He took the point of his knife and placed it between Alisha's breasts. He flicked the knife again and the flimsy undergarment fell away leaving Alisha's breasts exposed to the horrible gaze of Benny's stare.

"I knew those tits would be fuckin' beautiful," he said to Alisha.

"Benny, please stop this," begged Alisha. "Why are you doing this to me?" she sobbed.

Benny leaned over and took one of Alisha's nipples in his mouth and sucked on it so hard that Alisha started to scream. The more she screamed the harder Benny sucked. He then bit her nipple hard enough to make it bleed and Alisha could do nothing more than thrash about and cry to try and get this animal to stop hurting her.

Rick had come awake now and was wide-eyed at the sight he was watching. He tried to look away, but simply couldn't make himself do it. He was pulling for all he was worth on the tape that held his hands and feet fast to the chair. The harder he pulled, the tighter the duct tape became. He knew he couldn't get free, but he had to try.

Benny lifted his head from Alisha's breast and saw that Rick was awake. He stopped his sadistic abuse of Alisha's breast and walked over to Rick.

He came over to Rick and said, "Your father is worried about having lost a leg? Wait 'til he sees what I've done to you."

Rick had no idea what Benny was talking about.

"Shut the fuck up, Benny!" hissed Alisha.

Benny wheeled and slapped her right across the face. He hit her hard enough for it to smart, but not hard enough to bruise. He wanted her to still be beautiful when they found her dead body.

Once again he turned to Rick and said, "The big fuckin' deal, Dick Stuart, is gonna have a dead kid at the end of this day. That asshole Fastallo will regret the day he ever decided to take on Jack Ricco! I will continue to hurt people he loves until the day I die! I got Harry's Amber and now I'm gonna get his Alisha. I wish I coulda' fucked Amber the way I'm gonna fuck his Alisha."

Rick was not only scared to death right now but he was also confused.

What the hell is he talking about? he thought to himself. *He thinks that Dick Stuart is my father!*

Benny could see the confusion on the boy's face. "Oh, Ricky boy, they haven't even told you yet, have they? Oh, yeah, Dick

Stuart was fuckin' your mother when he was at Fort Sill, Oklahoma. The prick just walked out and left your mother pregnant. It all but tore her heart out," said Benny. He was enjoying the pain and confusion on the young man's face. He took his knife blade and placed it under Ricky's left breast. "Yup," he said, "just about tore her heart out."

He drew the knife blade under Rick's pectoral muscle. The knife left a trail of blood in its wake and caused Rick to scream out in pain.

"Something like this kid. I'll come back in a little while and make that cut deeper so I can really tear your heart out." This was said with such malicious detachment that it absolutely terrified Rick.

"Oh, man, I'm havin' a good time," said Benny.

He turned away from the thoroughly confused and terrified boy in order to pay more attention to the half naked Alisha. He grabbed her roughly by the hair and pulled her head to one side. He placed a kiss on her neck so roughly that she knew she would have a bruise on the tender skin where his lips had just been. He stepped back to admire his handiwork and noticed that Alisha's nipples were rock hard. They were not swollen from pleasure, but from the absolute fear and revulsion that had caused her skin to crawl from the attentions of this lust-filled animal she thought she knew.

She could see that he was fully aroused now. The sadistic treatment of her had caused him to go into sexual bliss. He was removing his pants now and Alisha knew it was going to get worse. When his pants fell to the floor, she saw that he was wearing no underwear and his manhood was filled with the cruel blood that was running through all of his veins now.

He came close to her. He started rubbing himself against her nipples. Her crying and begging him to stop seemed to make him even more excited. He grabbed her hair and pulled her face against him. Her tears and his own juices were causing delicious sexual pleasure for Benny.

"Fuck you, Fastallo!" Benny screamed.

He continued to rub his cock all over her face and breasts and all Alisha could do was sob and take it.

She knew that because of the increasing pressure as he rubbed himself against her, the end was close at hand. She knew that momentarily he was about to spend his filth on her and there was nothing she could do about it.

Suddenly he stopped. He backed away from her. He reached for a cigar that was on the table and began, with great ceremony, to light it.

"Do you wish you could do this to me?" he asked, obscenely licking his cigar. "Or maybe you wish that you could do this to me," as he cut the end off the cigar with a sterling silver cigar cutter.

Alisha just stared back defiantly. He was lighting the cigar now with one hand and rubbing his still swollen cock with the other.

"Now for my very favorite part," he said menacingly.

He moved close to Alisha's face and started to rub himself faster and faster. All the while he was puffing on the cigar until the tip of it was glowing red-hot. Alisha could do nothing more than stare at the hot tip of the cigar.

"Oh, God," cried Benny. "I'm gonna come!"

Suddenly a small red hole appeared in the middle of Benny Myers' forehead. The back of Benny's head exploded wide open and splashed bits of bone and brain across the room. Benny fell to the floor instantly dead. The cigar he was smoking lay across his chest burning a hole. He lay in a pool of his own blood under his head and a pool of his own sexual juices on his stomach.

The door burst open and a squad of the Miami SWAT team came rushing in.

A big black man came over to Alisha. He took off his jacket, wrapped it around Alisha, and said, "I'm Lieutenant Cobb, ma'am. You're gonna be alright now."

Chapter Thirty-Nine

Don Antonio listened intently as his lieutenant reported the circumstances of Ricco's demise.

"I see...yes. All right. "It is done, Joey...you get Frankie and catch the next plane back here," the Don ordered.

He then slowly lowered the solid ivory telephone onto its golden cradle and stared passively across his study. He was feeling melancholy for some reason as he studied the carving on the legs of the massive Italian provincial conference table that was the centerpiece of the room.

He muttered to himself, "What a pity that the porco, Ricco, died so painlessly."

He also knew from his conversation with Joey that there was no other option and that Lieutenant Cobb had paid his dues. The Don was grateful. Within four months Cobb had the extra bar that was promised.

Harry Foster, with a little guidance, could have been a Don. He was a manipulator of sorts but had class...so much so that he was able to steer others without them being aware of it. Perhaps "manipulator" was too strong, but he was usually able to get things done—his way, without ruffling feathers. At Fort Sill, when the "gang" was still intact, it just seemed that everyone fell in line with what Harry wanted to do on a particular evening. If somebody was short of money, it was Harry who convinced the group to chip in to help one of their buddies out. When it was just

Harry and Dick left, Harry made sure that Dick ate and drank free in whatever club he was performing at. Harry just had it in his genes. Not that he didn't make his share of mistakes, but he always learned from them and moved on. Harry commanded respect without asking for it. He probably missed his calling when the Army got him.

Harry had made a mistake when he assumed that Dick would acquiesce to his plan to rebuild the Realm in Oklahoma. He was hurt by Dick's tirade since he was only trying to get all his friends and their loved ones together, but he quickly rebounded by offering Brenda a position with the company.

He drew up a magnificent set of new plans to rebuild on the same site. Unknown to anyone, he had spoken on several occasions to Rick's high school baseball coach and ascertained that the kid had real potential. After getting his coach to forward some tapes of Rick in action, he made contact with the athletic department at the University of Miami, an institution he frequently supported financially.

Young Rick didn't know it yet, but as a result of showing the tapes to the right people, Harry had arranged a workout on campus at UM. And so he took Rick in for the "surprise" visit. All the chips were beginning to fall in place, just as he'd planned. As soon as Dick was healed, he would proceed with the master stroke.

Harry and Tommy huddled in the waiting area of the Emergency Room at Miami Dade General. Alisha and Rick had been brought in by ambulance ten minutes earlier. Alisha didn't appear to be in too bad shape…some scratches and the like, but Rick was a bloody mess.

His nose had been split and it required twelve stitches to close it, but miraculously, it hadn't been broken. Tommy was hanging on to Harry as if he was out of Harry's own nest, which warmed Harry's heart.

When Alisha came out, Tommy broke for her and clutched her as if he hadn't seen her in years. Harry followed and wrapped his arms around them both and knew that this is where he wanted to be and who he wanted to be with...forever.

In a moment, they turned collectively to see Rick standing in the doorway of the waiting room. The doctor came out and explained the treatment to his nose. He added that Rick had sustained a mild concussion and would probably be left with two black eyes. He agreed to release him after receiving assurance from Harry that he would get an appropriate amount of bed rest.

Harry felt sorry for Rick and so did Alisha. It was an awkward reunion, but Harry introduced Rick to Tommy. Tommy quickly endeared himself by telling Rick of his love of baseball. They all left the hospital, got into Harry's car, and headed to Key Largo.

It was quiet in the car. Everyone was exhausted. Alisha had discreetly informed Harry that Rick knew about Dick being his father. Harry's heart sank. He decided it would be best if everyone stayed at his place for the evening.

Since Brenda and Dick were unaware of Rick's visit, there was no urgent need to get to Key Largo Mercy until morning. There was a great deal of healing that was needed.

Alisha was on the brink of tears during the ride home. Harry was afraid to ask her what had happened, but he knew it would have to come out. But Rick...my God, what could he possibly say to Rick? He wondered during the drive if Rick even wanted to talk. It was still fairly early when they arrived at Harry's home. Harry had stopped on the way and had picked up some burgers and fries. They all sat down at the kitchen table and ate in silence.

As the evening progressed, Harry became even more concerned about young Rick. He didn't look good and didn't seem to want to converse with anyone. Harry recalled his personal experience at the Glade in Sebring several years earlier. He came to the conclusion that Rick needed some professional help.

Harry was concerned that his plan to bring Rick to Florida unannounced would backfire. How would Brenda feel about all of this? He decided that he needed to contact Brenda and Dick, bring them up to date, and see if they agreed that Rick was in need of some crisis counseling.

It was getting late and everyone felt that it was time to turn in. Tommy and Alisha went to their rooms while Harry escorted Rick to his. Rick said nothing and looked as if he were in shock.

After bidding Rick goodnight, Harry felt that he couldn't want any longer. He had to reach Brenda now and apprise her of the entire situation. It was 9:30 in the evening, so Harry rang Dick's hospital room, hoping that Brenda would still be there. He was in luck…Brenda answered the phone.   "Hey…sorry for the late telephone call," Harry said, "but I need to talk to you right away, Brenda."

She asked, "Are you coming over here?"

"No, I need to see you at my place. It's urgent," Harry stated emphatically.

It was twenty minutes later when Brenda rang the doorbell and Harry quickly let her into the house.

"What's this about?" she quizzed.

Brenda was wondering what was going on this late in the evening.

Harry invited her to sit down and she did so.

"Brenda, I need to tell you about what has happened today," and he began. The further he got into the story the more ashen Brenda became. At first anger began to flash in her eyes and cheeks and then the crying started.

"Oh, my God, Harry...how could you?" Brenda cried. "I want to see him right this minute!" she added vehemently.

Harry was able to convince her not to wake Rick if he was sleeping due to the concussion, but she insisted she wanted to look in on him. With much guilt and a heavy heart, he accompanied her to Rick's room.

Brenda eased the bedroom door open and saw an empty room and fluttering drapes at the window. Rick was gone.

Chapter Forty

Rick Just couldn't stand it. He had to get out of the bedroom and get away from these people. *Who the hell are they anyway?* he thought to himself. *I wind up with some psycho punching my lights out and the next thing I know he's tellin' me this guy Dick is my father.*

My father? he thought. *Could it possibly be...*

Summer of 1974...

"C'mon, Ricky! For Christ's sake, keep your eye on the God damned ball!"

John Mcleod was doing what he always did at Ricky's ball games. He was drinking beer and belittling Ricky's efforts at the plate. It was at times like this that Ricky hated his father.

Rick's father, John, was a soldier stationed at Fort Sill, Oklahoma. It was from Fort Sill that he was sent over to Vietnam and it was to Fort Sill he returned.

He didn't return the same way he left. He was unfortunate enough to be over in 'Nam when the '68 Tet Offensive took place. The North thought they could fool the South by hitting them with a sneak attack during a high, holy holiday in Vietnam.

It was a tactical failure, but an overwhelming public relations' victory. It was at that time that the American people decided to turn their collective backs on the men and women serving in the armed forces.

"It was the time of peace and love and bullshit," Mcleod would say.

"C'mon, Ricky, will ya?" Mcleod taunted.

One of the parents of one of the other kids said, "Oh, c'mon, John. Give the kid a break."

John Mcleod walked over to the parent, told him to "mind your own fuckin' business" and punched him in the mouth. That got John busted down to buck sergeant and caused a fight in the house that was colossal in scope.

"Why do you have to be such a loser, John?" asked Brenda. "Why can't you just be like normal fathers and complain about balls and strikes? Why do you have to torment your son? He's doing the best he can, and that's pretty damn good, by the way!" she added.

All John Mcleod said was, "My son? My ass, my son!" and out the door he went.

Ricky could hear his mother crying in her room from his room and went in to see if she was okay.

"You all right, Mama?" asked the boy.

Brenda looked up and held her arms out to the boy. He walked into them and although he wasn't quite sure what he was supposed to do, he let her cry on his shoulder.

It was after a while that she stopped crying when Ricky said, "Mama, what did Daddy mean?"

"About what?" Brenda asked.

"When he said, 'My son, my ass.'" And then quickly added, "I don't mean to use cuss words, but that is what he said, Mama."

If the boy had been older he would have seen the look of fear and frustration in his mother's eyes when she said, "Oh, don't pay any mind to Daddy when he's been drinkin'. He just sometimes says foolish things."

It was shortly after that, that Brenda and John Mcleod were divorced. Ricky never brought it up again and neither did Brenda. He always remembered it, of course, but really never thought there was anything to the remark. He just passed it off to drinking like his mama said.

Now, many years removed from John McCleod, he was sitting in a chair across from a man he had only just recently met and it was possible that this man, in fact, was his father. "Could this be?"

Rick just stared at the man asleep in the bed. He had been sitting by Dick's bed for over an hour and a half. Dick had been given pain meds and was dead to the world. Rick just watched his chest rise and fall and didn't know what to think. He didn't know whether he should hate this man, love him, or if he should be feeling any emotion in between. He was more confused than he had ever been in his young seventeen-year-old life.

He had grown up pretty much without a father since the divorce, but remembered thinking as a young boy that the other kids were lucky when it came to having somebody to play ball with or just throw a baseball back and forth with. He would feel very much left out when there were father-and-son nights at school. He always found one excuse or another not to play in any of the father-and-son baseball games.

I learned how to play baseball pretty good without one, he thought to himself. *All that time we spent in that shelter until Mama got that real estate business goin'. Where was he when we needed him? Where was he when all the other kids had fathers in the stands? Where was he when Mama was sick, but she still had to go to school and come home and take care of me?* All the years of being the kid who always took an uncle to the father-and-son games began to well up in Rick and it made him angry. *Where was this guy named Dick Stuart all these years?*

"I don't need a damn father now," he said out loud. He started talking as if he were talking to Dick, but Dick was deep asleep.

"All those years," he began. "I thought John Mcleod was my dad and it came down to where I hated him. I hated him because he was always making fun of me and fighting with Mama all the time. I hated him because he seemed to hate everything around him and there was nothing Mama or me could ever do that was right. I felt so guilty hating my own father and now I find out from a crazy man that he wasn't my father and that this guy lying in this hospital bed is my father. I don't know what to believe, and if it is true that he is my father, where the hell has he been for the past seventeen years?"

The tears were flowing freely down the young man's confused face. He was in a quandary that no seventeen-year old boy should have to deal with.

He started to get up to leave when Dick said, "Listen boy, I don't know if you are a dream or if it's the drugs, or if you really are here at my bedside. No matter what it is, I am going to tell you about the past seventeen years. I just need to start by telling you I only learned of your existence the day I met you in the driveway of your house. I looked at you and I was thunderstruck because I was looking into my own eyes, my own face, and perhaps I knew in that instant that I was looking into the eyes of my own son. It had to be because the instant I saw you, I fell in love. I fell in love with this vision of myself that I couldn't deny from the moment I laid eyes on you.

"I will tell you the story of the past seventeen years, but know this, young man—I love you with all my heart and if you'll give me a chance, I'll make it up to you somehow. I swear to God I will.

"I have always been a fighter. I never gave up on anything in my life, son. I was about to give up because of this leg, but now because of you, I will fight on against this and restart my life. This time however, with you in it, if you'll let me."

The boy just looked at Dick for the longest time. He wiped his eyes with his shirt sleeve and said, "Okay, I'm listenin', but I want you to know that I'm scared of this thing. It isn't every day that a boy gets a new dad."

That made Dick chuckle. He thought to himself, *That's my boy alright!* He then had to dry his eyes and said, "Okay, son, here goes…when I got out of the army…"

Chapter Forty-One

It was a night of great emotion that late evening in the summer of 1983. In room 511 of the Delray Medical Center, all the major players were in place, well past normal visiting hours. Tears fell like rain and no one was exempt. Harry, Brenda, Alisha, and Tommy had joined Dick and Rick in this odd reunion of sorts. Everything was out in the open now and all the guards were down.

Rick had bonded somewhat with his father and understood why Brenda had tried to conceal the truth. Dick had apologized to Harry for treating him so harshly prior to the accident and vowed to put his injury behind him beginning immediately. Brenda was crying with joy over the Rick's apparent acceptance of Dick as his dad. It was, indeed, a time for healing.

Dick also apologized for his failure to look over the plans Harry had left with him explaining that until now, he hadn't had the heart to look at them.

Harry told everyone there would be a time in the near future when all of them would sit down and look at the plans together, but the first order of business was to get Dick back on his feet. In that regard, Dick was to be fitted for an artificial leg in the next day or two and begin rehab simultaneously. They left to allow Dick to get his rest and all returned to Harry's home in the wee hours of the morning.

During the drive home, Harry informed Rick and his mother of the workout he'd arranged for Rick at the Miami campus.

Young Rick, already reeling from the events of the last twenty-four hours could not believe someone would do such a thing for a person he hardly knew, but then he remembered Dick's story and understood. Harry Foster was an unusual man…and so was Rick's dad. Needless to say, Rick, as well as Brenda, was elated over the prospects this opportunity afforded.

Harry was awakened by the ringing of the telephone early the next morning. *Too early*, he sleepily thought as he fumbled for the receiver.

"Hel…Hello," he answered halfway in a stupor.

"Enrico, my nephew…how are you this morning?"

Harry quickly became alert at the sound of his uncle's voice. "I'm good, Uncle Antonio, and how are you?"

"I am well, Enrico…forgive the early call this morning, but I have an urgent matter I would like to discuss with you at your convenience."

Harry knew that the "convenient" time for him would be right now. "Of course, Don Antonio, I am at your disposal," he replied.

"Good…can you meet me for dinner at my home this evening?"

"I'll be there, Uncle," Harry answered, knowing well enough not to ask why.

Harry rolled out of bed, made some coffee and showered. He wondered what his uncle wanted to discuss that was so urgent. He made a plane reservation for later that day and sat down to have his second cup when it hit him.

Oh, Christ…he wants a piece of the new club! he thought. *Oh, Shit!!!* Then he felt ashamed.

Here was a man that was always there for him and always would be. How could he refuse him? Besides…he knew the Don would not expect Harry to give him anything. The Don would invest. But how would Dick take it? He was still pondering that question when Alisha came into the kitchen and kissed him.

"Good morning," she said affectionately. "What a night, huh?"

It was a hell of a night as far as Alisha was concerned. Like everyone else, she had confronted her own fears during the previous evening. She had opened up about her harrowing experience of that day minus all the sordid details, in view of Tommy's presence. It was therapy for her and she had a good cry. She felt better this morning.

"Honey...I've got to go out of town on business today," Harry said.

"Was that the phone call I heard this morning?" asked Alisha.

"Yeah...look, hon, do me a favor and try to entertain the gang for me today as best you can," Harry said. "Let 'em sleep in. Maybe you guys could go have lunch or dinner with Dick at the hospital or something, huh?"

"Sounds good to me...any idea when you'll be back?" Alisha queried.

"I don't know for sure...my uncle wants to see me," he replied. "I'll call you when I know something," he concluded.

It was 6:30 that evening when the Don's limo drove through the electronically controlled iron gates of gothic design that led to the Fastallo mansion. The big Lincoln rolled around the expansive circular driveway and stopped in front of the main entrance of the estate. He was escorted to the front doors where the butler met Harry.

"Good evening, sir. I am Luigi. Don Antonio awaits your arrival."

Harry had been in this place on two occasions prior to this visit, both when he was a child.

It was big then, and it was just as big now, although Harry had much more appreciation for the furniture, fixtures, and art now as he followed the butler to the study. Joey was seated outside the huge mahogany pocket doors as was customary.

"Good evening, Enrico," Joey boomed as he rolled aside one of the heavy doors, after knocking lightly.

"Good evening...Joey, isn't it?" asked Harry as he entered.

"Enrico! It's so good to see you again," Don Antonio exclaimed as he kissed Harry lightly on his cheeks.

"Ah, but it is my pleasure as well, Uncle Antonio," Harry replied. Harry, as an instinct, always broke into the formal tone that was common when speaking to the Don.

"Please...sit with me and have a drink before dinner...what can I get for you?"

"I'll have what you're having, Don Antonio."

The Don pressed a button underneath the arm of his green leather chair and Luigi entered the study. "Two vodka martinis on the rocks, Luigi...very dry."

They soon toasted and had settled in with their drinks when the Don said, "So tell me, nephew, of the current events of the day. I have read much of the problems you and your partner have experienced lately."

Harry spent the next thirty minutes relating the entire story to his uncle, not knowing that much of what he told was already known by the Don.

"One thing that surprises me, nephew, is that you did not call on me for help with this situation," Don Antonio advised.

"Believe me, Don Antonio, there were times I wish I had, but I just felt that I shouldn't come running to you every time I bloodied my nose."

"I thought as much, Enrico...I thought as much. It is scary how much like your father you are. I guess that is why I love you so much," the Don added. "So are you ready to eat?"

Following the delightful meal of Maine lobster stuffed with shrimp, they settled back down in the luxurious leather chairs in which one could easily fall asleep. They each decided on a cup of chicory coffee to awaken their senses as it was getting late.

The Don began, "You know, Enrico, I have led this family for nearly forty years now and the business is getting so much more complicated these days...computers, drugs, law enforcement...it's getting hard for an old man like me to make a living." He continued, saying, "I've been giving serious thought to retiring...maybe moving to some place warm like Florida and enjoying my old age."

Here it comes, Harry thought. *The pitch.*

But Harry was wrong. He had completely miscalculated the reason for his visit to see his uncle.

"Enrico, you are the only blood I have left. I want you to take my place as head of this family..."

Chapter Forty-Two

Harry was absolutely astounded. This was the last thing he was expecting. His face blanched and for one of the few times in his life, he was absolutely struck dumb. He didn't know what to say.

"Enrico," started the Don, "I have watched you over the years and I see that you have a keen head for business and you also know how to get the most out every person in your employ. You have the kind of qualities that this position requires. You're graced with compassion, but not weakness. You are graced with strength, but you are not a bully. You are determined, but not pig-headed.

"In short, my dear nephew, you have all the makings of an excellent Don. The only question mark might be your ability to make the hard decisions when you may have to be harsh. I know from experience that you will only know if you have the strength when the time comes."

"Harry Foster, the head of the Boston family?" said Harry.

"Every person in this family and in every other family across the country knows that you are, in fact, Enrico Fastallo, my brother's son," answered the Don.

"Well, what about Joey?" asked Harry.

"He would be an excellent choice, but his leadership is not strong enough," said the Don. "He is a wonderful Consigliore. He is, however, best suited to be the number two man. He can give good advice when presented with all the options, but is not confident enough to decide what the options should be. I have trusted him with everything in this family, but I am not confident enough to leave the family to him."

"Is that fair to him?" asked Harry.

"It isn't a case of fair," answered the Don. "It is a matter of business and Joey would understand that."

"If you refuse me then I would turn to Joey as a successor, but I would be more confident with you as the head of the family. I am also being selfish by wanting to keep the Fastallo name at the top of this endeavor. If you accept this proposal, then we have much to do. I will have to show and teach you practically everything about this family's business. There will be people to meet and deals to be made, and it will take about a year for all of this to be done. If God grants me another year, that is," added the Don. The Don sat back and contemplated his nephew.

My God, he looks just like his father, thought Don Antonio. It was at that moment that the Don had his first doubts about his decision. He remembered the extraordinary lengths his brother had gone to in order to be disconnected from the family. He had gone so far as to change his name from Fastallo to Foster.

Oh my God, thought Antonio, *he will curse me from the grave if this comes to pass!*

He closed those thoughts from his mind and said aloud, "Well, my nephew, what do you say to all of this?"

"Uncle Tony," started Harry, "this is not a decision that can be made over dinner and a vodka martini, even though it was a perfect dinner and a perfect martini. I need some time to contemplate the enormity of what you are proposing.

"The decision is even more difficult because I have to make it completely alone. I can't reach out for any of the people I trust to help me. I am standing on the next to last step on the mountain and have to decide whether or not to step up that one more level. Nobody can counsel me because nobody can know about it. This to me is very very difficult."

DICK SWARTHOUT

The Don was pleased, but not surprised that Harry understood this side of this business he was in. "I do understand your dilemma, nephew," said the Don, "but this decision can not wait for too long a period of time."

"If my uncle would let me spend the night in one of his many bedrooms," answered Harry, "I will give you my decision in the morning. I doubt that I will get much sleep, so it needn't be your very best bedroom, Uncle."

"I am sorry to spring this on you so suddenly, but these things…"

Harry interrupted by saying, "Uncle Tony, no matter what decision I come to, this moment will be one of the proudest of my life. That you would consider me to try and fill the substantial shoes of Don Antonio Fastallo is an honor I could never even think of repaying."

"Then buona notte con amore, my nephew," said the Don.

"And with love to you as well," answered Harry.

The Don then stood up and opened his arms. Harry stood as well and walked into those arms and remembered back to when he was a boy. His uncle would always open his arms to Harry and Harry would always walk into them. He remembered how safe he always felt in that embrace. His uncle always smelled of cigar smoke and after-shave. His uncle still smelled of cigar smoke and after-shave, and Harry still felt safe in this man's embrace.

Could I possibly fill the space this man's absence will leave? Harry thought to himself.

True to Harry's wishes, the Don gave him the second best bedroom in the house. The most luxurious bedroom, of course, belonged to the Don himself. Harry let out a low whistle as he looked around the bedroom. It was huge. It had all the opulence that Harry had ever seen. He had spent $500 a night and not had rooms this magnificent. It was a darkly paneled room with dimensions of at least twenty feet by twenty feet. Harry thought back to his beginnings and remembered, "I've had apartments smaller than this room."

Everything about the room was soothing in order to facilitate sleep. The dark mahogany panels that made up the walls were laden with deep luxuriant oil paintings that were soothing to the eye. They were all of Italian pastoral scenes. Some were of Italian fishing villages and others depicted the great vineyards of the Italian countryside. There was a painting of an Italian table laden with fruits and magnificent Italian breads. The centerpiece of the painting was a gorgeous crystal decanter filled with deep red Italian wine. It was so beautiful that the person looking at the painting could almost smell the fresh bread and taste the robust wine.

The lighting was accomplished in two ways. There were overhead lights that had a dimmer switch next to the bed and on both nightstands beside the bed were magnificent, porcelain lamps. On the lamps were medieval figures done so delicately that one would swear they could see the figurines blink their eyes.

The centerpiece of the bedroom was a stately four poster bed of king-size dimensions. The covers of the bed had been turned down and a beautiful pair of silk pajamas were folded and placed neatly atop one of the overstuffed feather pillows. By a large chair close to the bed, slippers were placed on the floor and a large terry cloth robe was draped across the back of the chair. On the nightstand sat a pitcher of ice water and some fresh fruit. It wouldn't be polite for a guest to wake up thirsty or hungry in the middle of the night.

Harry sat on the bed and was dismayed because he knew that in spite of the comfort the bed was offering, he would get little sleep tonight.

He did, in fact, get a very good night's sleep. He had little trouble coming to his decision. Once his decision was made, and he knew himself well enough to know that he wouldn't change his mind, he slept like a baby.

It was morning now and he wondered how his uncle would take his decision. He had decided that he would turn his uncle down. He hoped his uncle would understand.

"So, nephew," the don started, "have you reached a decision?"

"I have, Uncle," said Harry. "I have to say no to your offer."

He saw his uncle's eyes narrow. Don Antonio had not heard the word 'no' too often in his lifetime. He was very much unaccustomed to it.

Harry pressed on. "I have my reasons and because of your generosity, I think you deserve to hear them if you would like."

"I would like that very much, my nephew. Why would you say no to your family?"

The last statement made Harry uncomfortable, but his mind was made up.

"One—you said last night that you would have to teach me practically everything in a year. That means that you would hold something back. The words 'practically everything' mean exactly that…almost everything.

"If I agree to learn almost everything, then that would mean that on some matters you would have to be consulted. You and I both know that a business can't be run with two bosses." Harry thought he saw the slight trace of a smile at the corner of the Don's lips.

He's awfully smart this nephew of mine. He would have made a fine Don, thought Antonio to himself.

"Two—I really do doubt my ability to make the hard decisions, as you so delicately put it last night."

The Don indeed did understand that one.

"And three," Harry went on, "I have a proposition for you."

Now it was the Don's turn to be amazed. "You have a proposition for me? What could that possibly be?" quizzed the Don. The Don could not hide his surprise.

"Uncle," Harry went on, "it is clear to me that you are ready to retire from this family business of yours. I don't believe that you are ready to plant grapes and eat oranges in the yard just yet. You are still a young man and still very healthy, thank God, and I don't believe you are ready to put yourself out to pasture. I think that you might like the challenge of a legitimate business. I intend to resurrect Another Realm into something even bigger than it was before. I also intend to open other clubs all over the country and Europe. I want to open clubs in Paris and in Rome first and then on to London. I need a man who understands the European mind and can get things done.

"If you will give this some thought, my offer is as follows: if my partner agrees with bringing you on board, then you will be given a third partnership in our company which, as you know, is called Brothers of Another Realm Incorporated.

"If my partner has any problem with bringing you on, then I am prepared to offer you half of my holdings, which would give you twenty-five percent of the company.

" I think with Dick and I back here in the states and you in Europe, we can't miss."

The Don then said, "How much will this venture cost me?"

"One dollar," said Harry.

"One dollar!" exclaimed Antonio. "What do you mean, one dollar?"

"Uncle Tony," began Harry, "do you really think that I am unaware of all the help you have given me over the years? Do you think that I don't know that you had people on the ground the instant you heard about the problem with Alisha and young Rick?

Do you really think that I am unaware of all the help I got when the construction phase of Another Realm was going on? Do you think I thought it was just a coincidence that I had no union and labor trouble at all? That material was always there and the prices were always as good as, if not better than, those anybody else in the area could get.

"Uncle Tony," said Harry, "make Joey your successor and be comfortable about it. He is a good man and his loyalty deserves this reward. Come with me in my new venture and accept this offer I make to you with a heart full of respect and love."

The Don then said, "You are my nephew, but you are your father's son. He was always the smarter of the two of us. He would have made a far better Don than I have been over the years. He decided back then, so many years ago, that this was not the life for him. It seems that after so many years of it, I have decided that it is no longer the life for me.

"You are right. I will name Joey as my successor. He will be a good Don. I will discuss with him my reservations about his ability to be number one and offer all the help I can give to him to make sure that it goes well. I will be sure to tell him that it was you who suggested to me that I was wrong and that I should go ahead with it and name him my successor.

"Go talk to your partner, nephew of mine. I will make my decision based on what he says."

Chapter Forty-Three

A week had passed since Harry returned from Boston and the memorable meeting with his uncle. He had checked in with Dick to see how the rehab was progressing, but did not get into any company business with him. This was a deliberate strategy on Harry's part, as he wanted nothing to interfere with Dick's scheduled release from the hospital.

Harry was pleased that the insurance company settled the claim on the fire. It amounted to nearly three million dollars and fully compensated the business for its losses. Although it was a substantial amount of money, much more funding would be necessary if Harry's plan for the new Realm was to become a reality. In this regard, he began to put out "feelers" for the capital and lines of credit that would be needed to get the project off the ground. After the Florida location was up and running, he was toying with the idea of going public in order to expand both nationally and internationally. But first, he would need to consult with Dick and his Uncle Antonio and get their input and advice on this strategy.

There was so much work to do and it was almost overwhelming to Harry. It seemed simpler to him when they had built the first one. Maybe it just seemed more monumental because Harry's plan for the new complex was much more involved, or maybe it was just the mere fact that Dick wasn't sitting across from him right now. His thoughts of Dick brought back memories of a much earlier time...

That crazy Dick would do anything for laugh. Harry had just landed a gig at the Holiday Inn in Lawton, Oklahoma. It was there where he would team up with Dale Carter, the ex-gospel singer who was performing in the lounge. In addition, Dick was tending bar in the club.

It was perfect…they were together and in their glory. It didn't take long for Dick and Harry to begin shouting insults to each other during Harry's sets, and soon Dale joined in the fun. This was all spontaneous, unrehearsed, and quite amusing to the club patrons.

The Inn management began to notice an increase in the crowds when Harry came on. Soon, an additional bartender was hired to handle the increase in business.

Harry smiled when he recalled that all that cavorting had developed into a segment in the show where Dick would stroll out from behind the bar, dancing with a mop as Dale introduced him as "the singing bartender." Dick would then join them for a couple of tunes, which were actually quite good.

"God! I miss those times," Harry thought. He was really missing the relationship with his buddy.

When Harry learned that Dick was to be released, he planned an elaborate party with Dick as the guest of honor and all of the Realm's employees attending. He had rented a banquet facility on the beach and arranged for a luau as well.

It was a wonderful gathering where almost all of the closest people in Dick and Harry's lives were with them. Dick was getting around so well that if someone didn't know better, he couldn't tell that he had an artificial limb.

As one might expect, Harry presented a wonderful homecoming speech, which welcomed Dick and also recognized Brenda and young Rick.

Without giving anything away, Harry tempted all of the employees with vague plans of new construction and that they would soon have their old jobs back, but in a more exciting venue. As the gala was winding down, Harry suggested privately to Dick that they meet sometime the following day and Dick agreed that they needed to discuss the situation.

They met the following day at eleven in the morning...just the two of them at an outdoor cafe near the beach and not far from the ashes and debris of the Realm.

As Dick expected, Harry had brought a roll of blueprints with him. After they were seated and ordered beverages, Harry began.

"Dick, I need to tell you about a trip..."

He didn't get a chance to finish the sentence before Dick interrupted.

"Harry...before you start, there's something I need to tell you. First, I want to thank you so much for your involvement in the lives of Brenda and Rick. It took their minds off a difficult situation and gave us all a chance to come together as a family."

Harry sensed something was coming. He knew Dick...something was up.

Dick continued, "You know, my friend, so much has changed in my life these past few months, that I sometimes can't fathom it myself. Being in the hospital for three weeks gave me a chance to think about things and my life as it is right now...about the things that are most important to me.

"You have been my closest friend for all of these years and you will always be, but Harry, it's time for me to move on."

Harry could see tears welling in Dick's eyes as he spoke. "Brenda, Rick, and I are leaving for Lawton in the morning, Harry. We're going to get married in a few weeks."

Harry looked away ever so slightly so as to hide the disappointment from Dick even though he was tickled to hear the news about the marriage.

"Harry, please understand that my life has been changed forever by the recent events and I want to be a father to my son and a husband to my wife."

Dick was crying...as the parting was hurting him as much as it was affecting Harry.

"Hey, guy," Harry said, "I fully understand and I feel kinda weird. I'm happy for you, yet I feel like shit that you're leaving. What are you going to do out there, Dick?" he asked.

"Well, I thought I would try to help Brenda grow her real estate company. And then watch my son play college baseball, hopefully near home."

"Who knows," Dick added, "Rick might be my first client in a new sports agency one day."

Harry smiled at that and said, "Yeah, man, wouldn't that be somethin'."

"Harry...I know you've probably got some ambitious plans that will require a lot of money. If you like, we can work out some kind of annual compensation spread out over a few years to complete your buyout of my part of the business. That should help you get the ball rolling a lot easier."

"Thanks, Dick...I might take you up on that," said Harry, still feeling like he was in a strange dream.

They sat there together for a few moments, each not knowing how to say goodbye. Finally, Dick arose from his seat and said emotionally, "Brother, it's been a hell of ride." He started to turn, but paused and said, "one more thing...will you stand for me at my wedding?"

Harry embraced him and whispered, "Of course I will."

Chapter Forty-Four

Harry knew that there was no arguing Dick's decision. He knew his friend well enough to know that he had made up his mind and trying to change it was like asking a baby not to cry. It just wouldn't do any good at all. He took Dick's decision with understanding, but it really broke his heart. He couldn't imagine running the Realm without Dick, but he certainly would try. He had discovered that he really loved the business world and was far more capable than he thought.

They got rip-roaring drunk that night. They reminisced and laughed and, in the manner that only men who are real friends can do, they cried.

It was true that from the very beginning of the relationship, so many years ago, the one thing they could do in front of or for one another was show their feelings. They trusted each other completely.

The stories were old, but they had never lost their luster for these two men. They were as fresh in their minds and hearts as if they happened yesterday. These experiences together were the fiber that made up the whole cloth of the relationship between these two old friends. It was a cloth as hard as canvas in its strength, but as delicate as Chinese silk in its beauty.

The next day, with a noble hangover, Harry boarded a plane for Boston. He had to go see Uncle Tony and tell him of the latest development and that it probably would put a kink in the plans to bring him on board.

Harry wanted to buy out Dick completely so that he would have a nest egg with which to work when he got back to Oklahoma. He just wasn't comfortable paying Dick back in a piece-meal fashion. He wasn't quite sure how this would go over with his uncle, but there was nothing else he could do.

The greetings were effusive as usual. "Enrico my boy, how nice to see you so soon," exclaimed the Don. "Do you have news for me?"

"I do, Uncle," said Harry simply.

They sat down at a long table in Don Antonio's dining room and began to talk. Harry related all that Dick had told him and confessed that he never even brought the Don's name up.

"It didn't seem to make sense at that point, Uncle," said Harry. "I knew that Dick's mind had been made up and I saw no point in muddying the waters."

Harry concluded by saying that he didn't think the plan could go forward because he felt that Dick had to be bought out totally right from the start. He explained to the Don of his discomfort with paying Dick off a little bit at a time.

The Don had been listening quietly, seeming to pay more attention to an apple that he had taken from a bowl of fresh fruit on the table. He was carving small slices from the apple and popping them into his mouth. He had a way of eating fruit that made anybody with him long for a piece of fruit as well. He somehow made the fruit seem absolutely delicious. He relished it as though it were something from heaven, which of course in an Italian's mind, fruit, bread, and wine were gifts from heaven.

The Don finally said, "Ah, Enrico, that's wonderful!"

Harry was perplexed. "I don't understand, Uncle Tony."

"How much do you think the buy out for Dick is?" asked the Don.

"Well," said Harry, "the insurance company gave us a check for three million dollars. I frankly think that Dick should be paid at least half of that for his end of the business; and then after that I'll have to come up with some substantial additional financing to even start the project."

"Enrico," said Uncle Tony, "I was intending to turn you down no matter what you said this morning. I must admit that this is the one scenario I never figured on. I know that your offer was based on love and respect and in gratitude for any help I may have given you. I will accept the love and respect with ease. The gratitude I will accept, but not in the form of a bill that is due and payable on demand. All that was done on your behalf was done out of the same love and respect that you give to me as my brother's son. I have the right to expect love and respect from you as my nephew, but you, too, have the right to expect it from me as your uncle. It is understood.

"It was from this understanding that I would have had to turn your offer down. I would not have been able to accept a third or a quarter of your company for free. I simply could not have done that. This latest development changes the whole structure of this thing."

The Don sat back, sliced another piece of fruit, offered it to Harry, and continued to speak as Harry accepted the offering. "Now here is my offer to you," he began.

"I will buy Dick out at the price of two million dollars. I will then arrange the financing at one half point over prime for the development of the rebuilding of Another Realm. You and I as partners will share in the responsibility of the repayment of this loan. It will be secured through normal and legitimate sources of finance and will be tainted with "family money" in no way.

"You will be responsible for fifty and one half percent of the loan and I will be responsible for forty-nine and a half percent of the loan. This is so because I want the company to stay in your control legally. I have been the last word on too many deals for too many years and I don't want that control anymore. It is one of the reasons I wish to retire from the business that I have been in for so many years."

Harry was thunderstruck. "Uncle Tony, you can't do that!"

His uncle stopped him with a raised hand and said, "Oh yes, I can, and oh yes, I will, if you accept my offer. I would suggest to you that you will not be able to get this kind of a financing package anywhere else and it would be foolish of you not to accept. I am willing to buy into your company, but I will not accept your generous offer to allow me to walk into it. What say you nephew?"

"Do you have any brandy?" said Harry.

"How about some Grappa?" said the Don.

"Grappa will be fine," said Harry. As if by magic Joey appeared with a lead crystal decanter filled with Grappa and two crystal glasses on a silver tray.

"Go get another glass, Joey," said the Don. Joey was confused, but as always, immediately turned to do his Don's bidding.

He returned within moments with the third glass.

"I think my nephew is about to offer a toast and I thought you might like to join us in it, my trusted friend," said the Don to Joey.

"Of course, Don Antonio," said Joey.

Harry smiled at his uncle and said, "To the brothers and the uncle of Another Realm."

Glasses were clinked and a small sip was taken by all three men of the pungent Italian brandy.

"I have a toast to make as well," said the Don. Don Antonio Fastallo then stood up.

Harry and Joey stood as well, following the Don's lead. "I raise my glass to you, Don Giuseppe Petringa."

The Don drained his glass and threw it into the fireplace, smashing the fine crystal to little diamond like shards.

Harry then did the same. "To you, Don Giuseppe Petringa." Harry's glass followed Don Antonio's glass into the fireplace.

Joey's mouth fell open and he fell back down into the chair he had been sitting on. He was dumb struck!

"Are you gonna drink that brandy or just hold it until it evaporates?" asked the Don.

"Don Antonio," started Joey.

He was interrupted, "When you talk to me from this day forward my name is Tony. It is you who are Don Giuseppe Petringa from now on."

The retiring Don took Joey's hand and kissed it in the normal show of respect for a Don by an underling.

Joey pulled his hand away as though it had been burned. "I don't know what to say to you, Don Antonio, other than thank you." He continued, "It will not be possible for me to call you Tony. I simply could not do that and I couldn't bear to be called Don by you. You will always be my Don and I will have to address you as such."

The Don smiled and said, "Well, okay, but only if you will allow me to call you Joseph from now on instead of Joey?" They laughed together and all agreed to these terms.

Chapter Forty-Five

The next few months flew by in tornado-like fashion. It was a complete whirlwind of activity and the days were not long enough. The financing of the complete package was accomplished by a consortium of banks from Boston to Rome with each of them taking a percentage of the loan. The money was completely legitimate, but it certainly helped that Tony Fastallo, in his days as Don Antonio Fastallo, had made many of the board members on all of these banks wealthy. They met no resistance to their financing needs. The total package was accomplished at an incredible speed.

All systems were go and venues of Another Realm were being built in Boston, New York, Chicago, San Francisco, Paris, Rome, and of course Key West. The plans for Dallas, Los Angeles, and London were already being designed.

The concept was the same in all locations. It was a series of different theme rooms, but in every one of the venues was a Jamaica Room in honor of Moesha. There was also a room in each venue that was indigenous to each area. For example, the Boston venue had a Tea Party room; the Chicago venue had a Slaughterhouse Room that featured the best steaks in the world; New York had the Broadway Room—and so on.

Tony Fastallo's ability in the world of legitimate business was as adept as his abilities as Don of the Boston family. He was also able to convince doubting Italians and French business people that this was a good thing to have in their cities.

He did such a good job that other cities were clamoring for venues as well. Milan, Italy, and the Riviera in France had all offered large tax incentives if Brothers of Another Realm Inc. would locate there.

The opening nights of all the locations were set for two weeks apart. That would give Harry the opportunity to rehearse the band on specialized material for each club and be available to appear at every opening night.

The wedding of Dick and Brenda was fast approaching and Harry made arrangements for everyone who had worked at the original Realm at the time it was burned out to be present at the wedding.

Harry paid for all the airfares and all the accommodations in Lawton, Oklahoma. The accommodations were provided by the Holiday Inn and the payback for Harry was a promise to come back for one night and do a performance in the lounge after all of the opening nights of the new clubs. Harry said he would do it if they could find Dale Cooper and Dick was made to tend bar that night. They agreed.

The day of the wedding was magnificent. The sun was shining and the sky was crystal clear blue. The sun took second place in brightness to the brilliance of the bride. Dick, of course, was as goofy as every bridegroom on his wedding day. He kept asking Harry, "You got the ring?"

"I have the ring," Harry would answer patiently.

"Do I look okay?"

"You look fine, now shut up! You're only getting married, for God's sake!"

The ceremony was beautiful, with Harry standing in as best man and Alisha standing up as Brenda's maid of honor. When the minister said, "Ladies and gentlemen, I give you, for the first time,

Mr. Richard and Mrs. Brenda Stuart." The applause broke out and everyone in the room was thrilled for both bride and groom.

Dick and Brenda started to walk down the aisle when Harry grabbed Dick by the arm and said, "Can you wait just a second, buddy?"

Dick was confused, but stopped in his tracks. "What's up, Har?"

Harry whispered something in Dick's ear and then to Brenda and all three of them broke out into a smile.

"Alisha," started Harry, "when Amber was killed I thought my life was over; and it really was until the day you came into my life. Being with you just plain makes me happy. I love you more than I could possibly tell you and I really want to spend the rest of my life with you. Alisha, would you consider marrying me? I promise I will do everything in my power to make you happy and be the best stepdad a man could be to Tommy. Alisha, darling, please, would you marry me?"

Alisha's eyes started to shine and brimmed with tears. "Harry, that's all I've ever wanted since the day I laid eyes on you. Of course, I'll marry you. When?"

Harry said, "How about right now, right here in Oklahoma where this journey of life for Dick and me began."

"I have asked Dick to be my best man and Brenda would agree to be your matron of honor if you would have her and I'm sure the minister and all the people in this church wouldn't mind going through one more ceremony for us."

The church burst out in tremendous applause and the minister just beamed his approval.

And so the Brothers of Another Realm were married in Lawton, Oklahoma, where it all began. It was a glorious day.

At one point during the reception Harry leaned over to Dick and said, "Hey, Dick, I got an idea!"